Paul growled, frustrated at the slowne. his own failure to get his message across. He threw back and stood up, hurrying to the little desk under the window. The computer was already on and he opened Notepad and began to type.

Matt, we've been friends almost our whole lives and I love you like a brother. I know that what you're saying makes sense but I know, deep down in my gut, that something weird and awful happened to me down there. I don't know what that stuff was, but it changed me somehow. I was alive, and then I was dead, now I'm alive again. I don't know what the hell's going on, but I think I might die for good soon and I have to get to Linda. She can't think that I just dumped her, stood her up, whatever. She has to know...

Matt, who had been reading over his shoulder, interrupted. "Dude, I'll tell her. Seriously. I'll make her understand what happened. But go to the hospital. Please. It's what Linda would want you to do." Tears welled up in Matt's eyes, which made Paul feel like crying, too.

No, he typed again. *I have to do this. If I'm going to die, I have to see Linda just one more time.*

First edition

Zombie

A Love Story

by PATRICIA LEE MACOMBER

Crossroad Press

CHAPTER ONE

Paul Tremblay—son of Marge and Joe Tremblay, employee of the New York City Public Works Department, only child, lover of all things caffeinated, idealist and romantic, future fiancé of Linda Gilchrist—that Paul Tremblay, woke up on a cold steel table in the morgue.

Slowly, as though his eyes were new and untested, he blinked away sleep—or whatever had possessed him those past long hours—and slowly drew his eyes over the scene around him. The room was large and empty, dimly lit and quiet. It smelled faintly of chemicals that Paul was sure had never been required in his life. Light bounced off of varying reflective surfaces and metal fittings.

Paul blinked again and rubbed his eyes. There was a dim light above him and beside the table where he lay was another table with another guy. No one else was around. In fact, the quiet—save for the hum of some machine far off in the distance—was almost…deafening.

First things first, Paul decided. He did a mental inventory of himself. He was covered by nothing more than a thin sheet and his skin sort of itched, though it wasn't really an itch. It was more of a faint irritation. That said, he seemed perfectly all right otherwise. The guy next to him…not so much. He was laid out, toe-tagged, and cut right down the middle.

Paul panicked. If the guy next to him was dead and sliced up like a Thanksgiving turkey, then surely that was his intended fate as well. He slid his legs over the edge of the bed—which really wasn't a bed at all, he realized, but a long metal table—and tested them for signs of failure. Nope! His legs seemed just fine too.

"Think, Paul, think!" he muttered to himself, sliding off the edge of that table onto the cool linoleum floor.

His legs held up under the strain, though when he took his first step, something dragged against the floor and pulled at his foot a bit. He glanced down at the offending cardboard bit, attached to his right big toe by way of a short piece of wire. His brow furrowed and he sat down on the table once more, hoisting his foot up to prop it on his left knee.

"A toe tag?" he muttered, frowning. "That means they think I'm..."

Panic raced through him again and he began twisting at the wire madly, not stopping until his toe had been released from the wire. He glanced at it, squinting in the feeble light to read his name, a long number, and nothing more. He tossed the tag away and stood up again.

He looked around the room once more, being careful to avoid looking directly at that poor soul on the table next to him. He spotted a bank of drawers, tables with medical instruments on them, a desk.

"Christ!" was all he could manage.

The table on which he had just sat contained a lower shelf and on that shelf was a bag, tagged with his name and number. He grabbed it off the shelf and dumped its contents out on the table. All his clothes were there, his wallet, cell phone and keys.

At that particular moment, Paul didn't care why he was in a morgue, how he came to be there, or any other damn thing. All Paul cared about was getting the hell out.

He pulled his clothes carefully over his naked form and eased his socks on over his feet. He saw that the wire from the toe tag had left a deep and lasting impression in the flesh of his big toe. He made a mental note to reference it later, during his law suit.

Shoes came next and then he thrust his worldly possessions into his pockets and strode to the door. He wasn't sure what was going on, but there was one thing he was certain of: He didn't want anyone associated with this place to see him; he wasn't about to let them stop him. Whatever had led them to think he was dead, he was very sure they didn't take kindly to corpses just up and walking away.

He pulled the large wooden door open and peeked through the crack. The hall was quiet; it seemed empty. Testing the waters, as it were, he pulled the door further open and stuck his head through this larger opening. Nothing.

With the all the courage he could muster, he stepped into the hall and began the long trek toward the exit. A sign on the wall proclaimed gratitude for donations made to Bellevue. So that's where he was!

He was halfway to the exit door when a woman clutching a large stack of files rounded the corner, headed directly at him. *Act casual,* Paul thought, and he pressed on at a leisurely pace. As he drew even with the woman, she pressed one hand to her mouth and made a face, turning her eyes away from him and hurrying past.

"What the...?" Paul grumbled. People here saw burn victims, lepers and other physical atrocities on a daily basis. What could possibly make her react so strongly to him?

When he reached that corner of the hallway, he drew to a stop in front of the convex mirror at the corner of the ceiling. Screwing up his face and his courage, he looked into it. Yep! That was his face, his hair...*God but I've got great hair!* he thought. But there was something else; something... gross.

Peppered across his face were a dozen or so dark patches, no larger than a nickel. They were more than merely dark; they were black. Black raised patches had sprouted on his face. He immediately swept his sleeves up and looked closely at his arms. A few of the patches were growing there, too.

"What the freak?" he growled, feeling the burn of panic rise in him again.

He hurried on with a renewed desperation. What in the hell had happened to him? The last thing he could remember, he'd been working. They had been finishing up inspections on the Manhattan sewer lines, getting ready for the re-build.

The exit lay directly ahead of him. Beyond that, people milled about a small waiting area and gathered at a nurses' station. Paul ducked his head and hurried. If they spied him, they might try to stop him and he wasn't about to spend one moment here that he didn't have to.

Twenty more steps and he was out the door into...darkness. Somehow, whatever had happened to him had kept him here for a while. The last thing he remembered was daylight. Now it was night, and Paul's eyes didn't seem to want to adjust to it. Neither did his mind.

His last coherent memories were of being at work, in those sewer lines, with...Matt! That was what he had to do. He had to call Matt and find out what the hell was going on.

Paul reached into his pocket and drew out his cell phone, still with half a charge. The familiar wallpaper blazed at him as he awakened the device. Linda. Linda's face had graced his cell phone and computer wallpaper since the day he had met her. In the beginning, she had been a pipe dream, a fantasy girl who somehow managed to end up in a fantasy marriage to him and who, through tricks of his own imagination, had managed to be happy about it. A year after meeting her, he was about to make that fantasy real.

Paul shook his head and tried to focus. Someone was coming out of the doors behind him and he slipped into the shadows cast by failing bulbs and full trees to avoid detection.

Matt was second on his contact list and Paul tapped the screen to dial the house. One ring, then two, then…

"Say words!" Matt was stoned. He always answered that way when he was stoned.

"Matt! God! I'm glad I got you."

"Hello?" Matt seemed confused.

"It's Paul, you goof. Listen…."

"Who is this?"

"Look, I just want to know what happened to me. We were…"

Apparently, Matt had checked his caller ID. "Dude, this is bogus. Totally not funny, Man. Paul is dead and you're using his cell phone to call me…"

"No! Listen, this *is* Paul. I'm not dead. I just…"

"Are you fucking crazy or something? This is a sick joke, using my best friend's cell phone to punk me! Calling me up in the middle of the night and growling like a …"

"Goddammit, Matt! Listen!"

The call ended and Paul's shoulders sank. The sound of laughter reached him and it made him sad. Why had Matt said that he was dead? Why couldn't he understand what Paul was trying to say?

"Growling?" Paul's face sank further into a frown and he shuddered.

Well, if he couldn't get anything out of Matt on the phone, he would just have to see him in person.

Having worked for the city for nearly ten years, Paul knew the streets of New York like the back of his very spotted hand. Spotted! *Were those there a moment ago?* He wondered. Images of disease of the week movies popped into his head, with the men in contamination suits gathering up and herding the infected. Was that what he was? The infected? Patient zero? He briefly entertained the notion that he might be walking the streets, infecting hundreds of people as he passed. That was just too ludicrous and he dismissed the idea as a product of panic.

He set off in the direction of his apartment. He and Matt had been best friends ever since fourth grade when Matt's mom had moved into Queens and dropped him into the public school system. Matt had been like a shot in the arm to Paul, who even then had taken himself too seriously. Matt was a goof, a class clown, a sometimes lazy-ass who never quite did well but always meant well. So, after graduation, Paul had taken an apartment with Matt, gone to work for the city to put himself through college, and two months later he'd managed to get Matt his first and only decent job.

One foot after the other, Paul plodded in the direction of their apartment. He didn't want the population at large to see him, so he avoided the subway and kept to the shadows as he walked. It was nearly five miles to their place, a long walk, but do-able. He picked up the pace a bit, desperate for answers.

New York City at night was, if anything, more lively than in the day. Bright blotches of neon color splashed across the sidewalk, flashing headlights strobed through the darkness. Paul had lived here all his life and there was nowhere on Earth he would rather be....except LA.

LA. That's where Linda was. He had met Linda at college and it had been love at first sight. She was blonde and gorgeous and smart. And the best part of all that was that she thought the sun rose and set on Paul. If they had been on a soap opera, they would have been a super-couple. He'd been studying engineering at NYU, she…English. Nine years later, he was finishing up his ten-year stint with NYC Public Works, in the hopes of getting a small pension. She had been offered a teaching position at UCLA, a promise of tenure in two years (English professors didn't seem to stay put for long) and the opportunity to work on her PhD.

So, Linda had gone ahead to LA with the idea that Paul would follow as soon as his ten years with the city were up. He only had two weeks to go. Damn the luck.

Paul passed the third ice cream store in as many blocks, his head low and in true New Yorker fashion, not meeting the eyes of anyone. So far so good. Another two miles and he could interrogate Matt.

Linda. His mind drifted back to her. A sudden stab of terror ripped through him as he remembered the ring he had bought her. They had lived together for four years and he had been about to propose when the offer came in from LA. So, being the cautious and wise man that he was, he had tucked the ring away with the idea that he would propose to her as soon as he made the move to Cali, and then only if their relationship survived the separation. That ring was now neatly tucked into his underwear drawer.

One more mile. A finely-dressed lady with an equally finely-dressed little boy passed him. As they did so, the child looked up and caught sight of Paul's face. The boy tilted his head and scrunched up his face, then made the proclamation: "Eeeew!"

Paul turned his head away and frowned again. For a naturally happy guy, he sure was frowning a lot.

Two more turns and Paul was staring at their apartment building. It was short and squat, converted from an old Brownstone. It still bore the bomb shelter sign that had been posted there in the sixties. He fished out his keys as he approached it, his mind spinning circles around the questions he had.

He let himself in the front door and took the stairs to the second floor, where his apartment awaited him. The key slid home and Paul turned it, listening to the gratifying turn of the tumblers inside. He pushed the door open a few inches and met resistance.

"Matt! Hey, Matt!" he called in through the crack in the door. He was rewarded with the sound of footsteps within.

Matt's eye appeared in the crack of the doorway, heavy-lidded and blinking stupidly. He was, indeed, stoned. "Paul? Oh my God!"

"Undo the chain, Matt. Please."

"Dude...you're dead." He said it more as a matter-of-fact than as a threat.

"Matt, I'm not dead. I promise. Now, please, open the door."

The door slid shut and Paul heard the sound of metal against metal. Matt pulled the door open and blinked rapidly at him. "Is it really you?"

"Of course it's me, you doofus." Paul chuckled and moved to hug him. Matt backed away.

"The paramedics told me you were dead. They hauled you away."

"Well, I'm not dead. Obviously, they were wrong." Paul paused, wanting this to sink into Matt's drug-addled brain. "But you have to tell me what happened."

"Dude, you look like shit." He moved aside as Paul made his way deeper into the apartment. "Your face is all fucked up and...why are you making that sound?"

"What sound?" Now Paul felt anger welling deep in the pit of his stomach. "Tell me what happened."

Matt took another step backward. "You may not be dead, but you look like death warmed over. Seriously, man, you should really be in a hospital.

I think you've had a stroke or something."

"I haven't had a stroke and I'm not dead." Now, he was yelling. The frustration had a choke-hold on him and he couldn't manage to calm himself. "But I need you to tell me what happened."

Matt blinked stupidly.

"Are you hearing a single word I'm saying?" He took one step toward Matt and watched his friend's face pale.

"I think I should take you to the hospital. You need some help." Matt proffered his hand, palm up, to his friend.

Paul looked at the hand, then back to Matt. His chin sagged to his chest. "I…just need…to know what happened to me."

Matt's tone was softer now, more sympathetic. "Paul, you look like shit. And I can't understand a word you say. Please let me get you some help."

Frustrated beyond anything he could remember, Paul did something so uncharacteristic that it scared even him. He lunged forward and grabbed Matt by the shoulders, shaking him hard and screaming. "I don't need help! I need answers! Now, shut the fuck up and tell me what happened to me, dammit!"

Matt whimpered, winced, and pulled away from him.

"Oh God! I'm sorry. I'm sorry!" Paul let him go and backed away, feeling the hot sting of tears and guilt well up in his throat. He sank into the chair and let his head fall into his hands on the dining table. "I'm just so… scared."

After a few seconds, he lifted his head slowly and looked across the table. An old pizza box lived there, along with his dirty coffee mug, a magazine, two pens and a legal pad with some scribbling on it.

Paul grabbed the pad and one of the pens and began to write furiously. *I can't remember what happened. Tell me,* it said.

He shoved the pad in front of Matt's face and raised his eyebrows.

Relieved, he watched as Matt sank into the chair next to him. "You really don't know what happened to you?" Paul shook his head and Matt nodded. "Okay, I'll tell you what I know."

Paul tried on a smile, which must have come across as more of a sneer because Matt made a face and looked away.

"Okay, so we were working down in the tubes out where they're doing the renovations. You know, the sewers that run past all those factories and shit? We were almost at the end, taking those readings. *Last one of the day,* you said. There was this big pile of old trash from when they had originally built those sewer lines and you had to climb over it to get to the other side and take the readings. You wouldn't let me go because you said I was too clumsy and I would rush it.

"Anyway, we were talking and you got over the top of that rubbish, still talking. Then you said something about it being really gross over there and something about a puddle of blue goo. You cursed when you stepped in it. I remember because I laughed and made a joke. You know, 'Some days you step in it, some days you don't.' Then you came back over the top of the trash and you were all covered in that blue shit.

"So, we walked back to junction eight-twenty-three and climbed up and out. The stupid blue stuff glowed in the dark down there, but once we got topside, it was gone. We were walking back to the truck when you doubled over. You dropped straight to the ground and started rolling all around like a dead fish or something. I called nine-one-one and by the time the EMTs got there, you had stopped having fits. But they said you were dead.

"Dude, they put you in a body bag and hauled you off to Bellevue. I followed just to make sure they weren't screwing up, but the doctor came out and told me you were dead. He said they didn't know what of, but that you were just dead. They asked me if you had any next of kin and whatnot. I gave 'em your parents' number. Man! I wish I'd have known you weren't really dead. Did they screw up or something? What's going on?"

Paul scribbled hastily. *I don't know. Linda?*

"Linda? Oh, Linda. Right. Naw, I don't think nobody called her. I didn't have her number, but I was gonna go through your cell phone once they released your stuff and call her."

Don't call Linda, Paul wrote quickly. He thought for a moment and Matt seized that opportunity to offer what might have been the only sound advice he would ever come across.

"Dude, you need to let the doctors look at you and figure out what happened."

It was Paul's turn to blink. That was the sane thing to do, he realized. But something deep in the pit of his gut told him he shouldn't do that. *No,* he wrote. *Got to see Linda.*

"But Dude, you've only got ten work days until you get your pension. Just see a doctor, huh? Maybe they can help you. And man, whatever that shit is on your face, it looks like it needs some help."

Not going to last that long, Paul wrote and suddenly he felt like crying.

His grandmother had told him that everyone knows right before they're going to die. That was five hours before she died. Paul knew, too. *Got to get to Linda. Tell her I love her.*

"Paul, she knows that. Just please get some help."

Linda has to know. I didn't abandon her.

"Okay, call Linda."

No.

"Call her. Then go to the hospital."

No.

Matt sank back in his chair with a worrisome frown. "You're my best friend. My BFF, dude. If anything happens to you..."

Paul growled, frustrated at the slowness of hand writing everything and his own failure to get his message across. He threw back the chair and stood up, hurrying to the little desk under the window. The computer was already on and he opened Notepad and began to type.

Matt, we've been friends almost our whole lives and I love you like a brother. I know that what you're saying makes sense but I know, deep down in my gut, that something weird and awful happened to me down there. I don't know what that stuff was, but it changed me somehow. I was alive, and then I was dead, now I'm alive again. I don't know what the hell's going on, but I think I might die for good soon and I have to get to Linda. She can't think that I just dumped her, stood her up, whatever. She has to know...

Matt, who had been reading over his shoulder, interrupted. "Dude, I'll tell her. Seriously. I'll make her understand what happened. But go to the hospital. Please. It's what Linda would want you to do." Tears welled up in Matt's eyes, which made Paul feel like crying, too.

No, he typed again. *I have to do this. If I'm going to die, I have to see Linda just one more time.*

"I'll call her for you. She'll come. She loves you and she'll come. Then you can go to the hospital, huh?" Matt was all-out crying now and it made Paul sad beyond words.

Nononononono! Paul typed. *You have been a great friend, and I know you mean well, but I have to do this. Don't blame yourself. Honestly, none of this is your fault. I just have to see Linda. Have to.*

Paul stood up and headed down the hall toward his room. Matt followed close on his heels, blubbering and talking a mile a minute.

"Please let me get you some help. Don't do this."

Paul rummaged around in his underwear drawer until he found the thing he was looking for. He held up the small blue velvet box and smiled, then tucked it neatly into his pocket and shut the drawer.

"What if you die on the way there? Huh? You'll never get to see Linda and you'll be dead. Maybe for real this time. If we go to the hospital first, that way you can maybe get some help, *then* see Linda and maybe live happily ever after. Huh? Doesn't that sound better?"

Paul shook his head and marched back down the hall to the computer. *Taking the car,* he typed furiously. *Tell my parents that I love them.* He rose from the chair and headed for the door.

With all the courage he could muster, Matt stepped in front of him. "As your best friend, I cannot let you do this." He waved the cordless phone in front of Paul's face. "I'm calling nine-one-one and I'm getting you some help, whether you like it or not. You'll thank me later." Matt pushed the ON button.

Paul batted one hand in Matt's direction, sending the phone flying across the room. Matt watched it go, his expresion caught between terror and determination.

It was all determination when he turned back to Paul. "I've still got my cell phone. Ha! What do you think about that?"

Paul uttered something of a growl and snatched the phone from Matt's hand. He turned to the doorway again. Within seconds, he was through the door and partway down the hall.

"Fine!" Matt yelled after him. "I'll just wait until you're gone and then call for help. Yea, buddy! I'll report the car stolen. Then they'll catch you and get you to the hospital. I'm not letting you die, man! You hear me? I'm not letting you die!"

Old Mrs. Carter across the hall stuck her head out the door, sporting a moo-moo and a mean expression.

"Sorry, Mrs. Carter," Matt mumbled, lowering his head and ducking back into the apartment. He went to the window then, and watched as Paul pulled out of the parking space far below and out onto the street.

CHAPTER TWO

Paul was a man with a plan. He needed to see Linda, yes, but there were other things that needed doing. Everything Matt had said was true: He needed to see a doctor, should go to the hospital, could easily let Matt call Linda for him. But something drove him—something he couldn't explain—to see Linda in person. Something beyond comprehension told Paul that he wasn't going to last long, and that he had to get to Linda.

First, though, he needed to go back to that sewer and see for himself exactly what it was that had taken him out. First the sewer, then a hasty exit. He only prayed that he would make it out of town before Matt reported the car stolen and the police caught up to him.

The particular point in the sewer line where he and Matt had been working was in the industrial section and Paul pointed the car in that direction. He drove just fast enough to get there quickly; not fast enough to attract attention and get pulled over. Paul had spent a good portion of his adult life debunking the myths that circulated about the sewers. No, there was no giant alligator. No wild band of mutant humans lived there. There were no toxic waste dumps, no ravenous zombies, and no packs of wild rats with super-human intelligence. As it turned out, he seemed to have been wrong about at least one of those.

He guided the car across the bridge and into the industrial section. He turned his lights off and eased up to the access point near an old abandoned warehouse. There were plenty of those in the city lately, out-sourcing being what it was and all. This particular one had made cleaning solvents for the avionics industry and the military. It, along with several other companies on that block, had ceased operations about five years back.

He kept the headlights off, running dark, pulled up next to a derelict eighteen-wheeler and turned off the engine. As he stepped out of the car, keys in hand, his left leg almost gave out on him. He gasped a bit and put one hand on the door to steady himself, then pulled himself upright.

It had been a long night and his mind—if not his body—was tired. Slowly, he made his way toward the entrance to the sewers, a manhole some forty feet from the back yard of the place. As he went, he toed through some discarded trash which peppered the ground, hoping for a jar with a lid still intact or something like it. Three feet shy of the manhole, he found a small applesauce jar, its lid lying next to it, unbent. He plucked it from its resting place and popped it into his pocket. All he wanted was to get a sample of this stuff and somehow find out what it had done to him.

Manhole covers, by and large, are heavy things. On work days, Paul and Mark carried pry bars to help lift them. Paul had no pry bar that night, so he had to settle for wedging one finger into the little hole. He braced his feet against the packed dirt and tugged and hauled at it until he had moved it a few inches out of place. Then, with a surly grunt and a small squishing sound, he heaved it over and out of the way.

It was dark down there and Paul didn't have a flashlight tonight. It became painfully obvious to him that he'd jumped into this unprepared, had not clearly thought it all through. Whatever.

He slipped into the hole and let the darkness devour him. Somewhere off in the distance, a woman screamed. Probably a mugging, Paul told himself. He felt his feet touch solid concrete and he let go of the ladder.

A small circle of moonlight shone above him and it made the puddles at his feet sparkle and shimmer with borrowed light. Ahead of him, a deeper, brighter glow emanated from the far end of the tunnel. It was partially obscured by the hill of trash, of course, but Paul could still see it. He shivered.

Armed only with his own meager night vision and a decent center of gravity, Paul shambled toward that blue glow. It emanated from a point only fifty feet or so in front of him and with each step he took, he felt his skin tingle and chill.

He took more care climbing over the trash this time, simply because he couldn't see anything and he feared that a misstep could cause him more injury than he had already suffered.

Once on the other side, the source of that blue glow became evident. A large puddle of liquidy goo covered the floor of the tunnel. Spatters of it had coated the walls and continued to ooze down out of the pipe above. Paul kept close to the right-hand wall, away from the sticky, glowing trail of goo. Cautiously, he made his way to the edge of the puddle, stopping just shy of its edge.

The stuff just soft of sat on the water. It didn't actually float, but rather coated the surface, as if pinning it down, holding it captive. Paul reached into his pocket and pulled out the jar, meaning only to take a small sample of the spill; just enough for testing.

When he placed the jar at the edge of the stuff, taking great care not to let any more of it touch his skin, the blue goop seemed, very literally, to crawl into the jar. The rim had just sunk below the surface of the standing water when the blue stuff lurched forward and rushed in. No water went with it and Paul frowned, wondering whether the goo was alive, or whether his addled brain had simply misinterpreted the physics.

He held the jar up to his face and studied it. It was blue, translucent and thick. No water had entered the jar and so what he had as a sample was pure blue goo. Quickly, he placed the lid on the jar and torqued it as tightly shut as he could. Then he placed the jar back in his pocket and turned to mount the pile of trash and make his way out.

Letting the small circle of moonlight be his guide, Paul headed for the ladder and sweet, fresh air. He had become painfully used to the dank, acrid smell of the sewers, so it never really bothered him. But he remembered Linda's reaction on the few times he had come straight home from work without stopping at the dispatch station to bathe. She'd wrinkled her nose and turned away, pressing one hand to her mouth and shutting her eyes. Not one word had she uttered. She's just pointed at the bathroom and gagged a bit. He'd done it twice early on, and then never again since.

It was no small feat to haul himself up that ladder and out of the hole. For some paranoid reason he couldn't quite fathom, he felt it was absolutely imperative to shut that manhole. Perhaps the goo would escape and infect others. Perhaps it was a sentient sort of thing and would go on a rampage throughout the city.

"Stupid!" Paul grumbled at himself. "You're being stupid."

Then he thought about how the stuff had crawled into the jar. He flipped the manhole cover onto his back and slid it back into place, listening as the grating sound of metal on metal echoed through the empty industrial district. Then he stood and, as quickly as he could manage, made his way to the car.

He wasn't sure if Matt had actually made good on his threat, but he was willing to bet money that he had. That meant that Paul had to get out of the city as quickly as possible; before the police could spot the car and stop him.

He would worry about taking his sample to the hospital later. For now, all he wanted was to see Linda and feel re-assured that she still loved him, and he was a long way from Los Angeles.

CHAPTER THREE

Paul watched as New York City grew ever smaller in his rear view mirror. Ever since he had left the apartment, he'd waited for those flashing lights to appear in his mirrors. Matt was a good friend and he knew that he was only concerned for his safety. Most people saw Matt as a dolt, a ne'er do well, a waste of oxygen. Most people didn't know Matt. The man had a good heart and he was as loyal as the day was long, but he was rough on the surface, and most people didn't take the time to get to know him.

Matt was the son of an alcoholic and some unknown condom-challenged one night stand. He'd practically raised himself and at the same time had taken care of his mom, until she died of alcohol-related diseases when he was fourteen. After that, Matt had gone into the system for a month, until Paul's parents had completed the paperwork necessary to foster the boy.

Paul hadn't been kidding when he said he thought of Matt as a brother. Together, they had survived some close-calls, pulled some epic pranks, and in general held each other together through everything. He knew Matt blamed himself for not going over the trash pile. He knew Matt was only trying to protect him and help him. Still, he couldn't let anyone, not even Matt, stop him from getting to Linda.

The light of the city glowed brightly in his mirror. Ahead, there were thousands of miles of highway. A sudden thought assaulted Paul's mind and he nearly threw on the brakes. He had no idea how to get to LA.

The car he was driving was only a year old. He and Matt had bought it together. They had invested $5000 of their own savings in it, and then gotten a loan in Paul's name to cover the rest. Paul had paid ahead on it, gotten the loan down to almost nothing. He had intended to give the car to Matt when he left for Cali.

He eased the car off to the side of the road and put it in park. Linda's address was emblazoned on his memory, so he punched it in to the GPS and waited. There was hardly any traffic at this hour and he hoped that Matt hadn't made good on his promise to report the car stolen. If he had, there was nowhere to hide.

The GPS beeped and a map appeared. Paul smiled and pushed the shift lever back into drive. He eased back onto the road then, following the map and shaking his head at the voice. Why did these things always have the most pretentious voice possible?

Paul drove on, sticking to the speed limits and keeping a careful eye out for cops. He felt fairly sure by now that Matt had not called them. He could picture his friend pacing back and forth in the apartment, trying to decide what the right thing to do was. The odds were very good that Matt had continued pacing, probably smoked another fat one, and then fallen asleep without any decision having been reached. Classic Matt.

Paul passed the state line and kept going. A thin slit of sunrise spread across the back window. He would need to stop for gas soon, but for the moment he was good and he kept driving.

Linda felt the vibration of the alarm transfer from the nightstand to the bed to her cheek as it lay on the pillow. That more than the noise of it woke her. She reached out, letting her fingers feel the items on the nightstand—cell phone, bottle of aspirin, book, tissue box—and finally found the alarm. She pressed at several buttons, got it wrong, finally found the right button, and the alarm went silent. The button slapping was why she had to reset her alarm clock every night. She was not a morning person.

She threw back the covers and slipped her feet to the floor immediately. If she didn't do that, she ran the risk of falling back asleep. Her first trip was to the bathroom, where she yawned continuously as she peed, brushed her teeth and washed her face. She hated morning breath, hated it more than anything. Her day just couldn't go on until she had scrubbed it away.

Back to the bed then, where she sat down and pulled the cell phone off its charger. She stopped for a moment while she yawned some more. God, how she wished it was Saturday. The next part of her day had been a ritual since the day she had left New York. No day started or ended properly without her talking to Paul.

Paul. He was thousands of miles away and oh Lord, how she missed him! The look on his face when he first woke up, like he was always surprised she was there. The joy that overtook his eyes when he realized that she was, that she was his, and that would never change. She loved the cute way he had of eating his cereal. He ate it dry with a spoon, then took a swig of milk from a glass after every bite of cereal. He said putting it in milk made it mushy too fast. His way kept it crunchy longer. She wondered to herself if their future children would eat their cereal that way.

Smiling as though her face might split open, she almost squealed with joy as she thought of Paul. He was her love, her buddy, her everything. She had dated other men briefly; rich men, handsome men, brilliant men, handsome men who were rich. But Paul was THE ONE. He wasn't handsome or rich or brilliant, but he was sweet and loving and funny and giving.

She shivered, sighed happily, and rested back on the pillows. Paul was number one on her speed dial. She pushed the button and put the phone to her ear, waiting for his sweet voice.

Paul's phone rang. The sound of it made him jerk the wheel and he nearly cried out. He had seen far too many accidents come from talking on the phone while driving, so he made it a personal rule that he would always pull over before answering. To that end, he steered the car to the breakdown lane and put it in park.

Linda. It was her ringtone. He tapped the screen and pressed the phone to his ear.

"Hello?"

"Paul? Is that you?" Her voice sounded concerned. Had someone called her to tell her of his plight?

"Good morning, baby," he said and waited.

There was a long silence and then, "Are you okay? Why are you making that noise?"

"What noise?"

"Are you sick or something? Did you lose your voice? Do you have a sore throat?" She sounded nearly panicked now.

"No, I'm fine. Listen…"

"Okay. I guess you're sick somehow. Cough once for laryngitis, twice for strep."

Paul made a face and then decided to err on the side of safety. He coughed once.

"Poor baby! I'm so sorry you're sick. Anyway, this is just my usual morning call to tell you I love you."

"I love you, too, honey."

"Huh? I'm sorry, baby. I don't understand anything you say." There was a little titter of laughter and she continued. "I know you can't talk, but I love you anyway. I just wish I was there to take care of you."

Why oh why couldn't she understand him? He was speaking clearly enough. He could hear it. "I'm coming your way, Linda. I couldn't wait any…"

"I know it must hurt to talk. So, you get some rest, do what the doctor says….you have been to a doctor, haven't you? Of course you have. Anyway, get some sleep, take your meds and rest your voice. And if you get bored, just think of you…and me…and that cozy little inn we went to that summer…" She broke off in a squeal of erotic self-pleasure. "And remember, I love you times infinity. Email me." She made kissing noises and ended the call.

Thoughts of that inn always got Paul heated up, too.

He looked down at his crotch.

Nothing.

Damn!

He put the car back into drive and pulled onto the freeway again. Linda had called him every morning since she'd been gone. And every day on her lunch break. And every night to say goodnight. Sometimes, she called him with good news and sometimes he called her when things weren't going so well for him. All in all, they probably spoke more now than when they lived together. The sound of her voice, he always told her, was like a visit to Heaven.

Another hour of driving found the gas gauge almost to "E". There was a sign up ahead listing the gas stations and food stops at the next exit and Paul turned on his blinkers. The sun was low in the sky and a soft pink glow illuminated his field of vision as the sun in the east reflected off the buildings coming up in the west. He guided the car into a large gas mall, one of those places that try to satisfy the traveler's every need. There was gas, a convenience store, and two chain restaurants, all neatly tucked into one smallish building.

Paul eased up to the pump and turned off the engine. It was still daytime, and that allowed people to more easily see his affliction…whatever it was. He glanced in the mirror and was pleased that there were no new spots and the old spots had gotten no larger. It's not like he could do anything about them, but at least it didn't seem to be worse. Short of putting on a ski mask and being arrested for attempted robbery, he had no options.

He slipped out of the car, keeping his head down and hurrying to fill the tank. He swiped his card and removed the nozzle, then held down the handle as the gas flowed into the tank.

Most people, when confronted with someone who has a disease or deformity, will politely look away out of a sense of guilt. This was not the case with the large man at the other side of the pump. He had food stains on his t-shirt and a day's growth on his face, so he was no prize himself. On catching sight of Paul's face, he leaned forward, squinted, and tried to get a closer look. Paul turned, placed his back to the man and willed the tank to fill faster.

The man moved again, peering at him from the other side of the pump and taking a step closer. Again, Paul moved so that the pump was between the two of them and again the rude man shifted his position to get a better look.

"Back off, okay!" He growled and suddenly a film clip played in his brain. *The Elephant Man, starring Paul Tremblay.* He shook off the image and tried to ignore the man.

Finally, the pump shut off and Paul replaced both the nozzle and the gas cap. Then he got into the car and pulled it around to the little parking area behind the building. Countless family road trips had taught him to take care of business when you had the chance. His father's lectures to that effect were so ingrained in him that it was almost a habit. Get gas, take a leak. To that end, he ducked his head and trotted toward the rest room on the side of the building at a rapid pace.

Once inside, he felt more at ease. There were no prying eyes here, no accusing stares. He thought once more of *The Elephant Man* and a shudder raced up his spine. He unzipped, sidled up to the urinal and prepared himself mentally.

Nothing.

He tilted his head to one side and tried to remember the last time he had urinated. Yesterday. Before they had left for the sewers, both Paul and Matt had taken a bathroom break. So that would have been the last time he had relieved himself. Even accounting for the fact that your body...

Wait just one little minute here! he thought. *If your body completely evacuates when you die, how come my pants are clean?*

That simple thought froze him where he stood. Your body pushed everything out of it at the moment of death. He knew that to be true because of when Matt's mom had died...another of those memories that made him want to gouge his eyes out. So if he had died, how come there were no stains on his pants or his underwear.

"Okay, okay!" he grumbled at himself.

He cleared his mind, shut his eyes.

Nothing.

One hand reached out and turned on the water. Hey, it had worked when he was little.

Nothing.

"Really?!" He offered open hands and looked to the ceiling. "My pecker doesn't work? It makes my pecker not work? Whatever *it* is!" First he couldn't get wood when he was thinking about Linda and the inn, now he couldn't take a leak. "Oh come on!" he yelled and slammed his hand against the cheaply tiled wall.

He was rewarded by the sound of cracking bones and shifting flesh. He pulled his hand into range and stared at it as if it were some sort of alien being sent to destroy him. The fingers were twisted oddly and his knuckles seemed flattened. There was no pain. He raised his other hand and set about putting things back where they belonged, which also caused him no pain.

Scared and completely rattled by this new turn of events, he headed for the door. At the last second, he realized that he was still unzipped and flapping in the breeze, as it were. He quickly fixed this little problem and made for the car. It wouldn't do to be arrested as some sort of flasher or something. What would Linda think?

Paul guided the car through the maze of pedestrians, other cars, and traffic signals and back onto the freeway. Every now and again, he glanced at his hand as though it might fall back into a state of disarray. It stayed in its current condition, however, and Paul felt his spirits lift briefly. Then his phone rang again.

It was Matt's ringtone and he ignored it. He couldn't seem to make Matt understand him anyway, so what was the point?

His mind returned to his previous question. If he had died, why, then, were there no stains on his clothes? Surely, the people at the morgue had not taken the time to clean his clothes before putting them in that bag. They hadn't even gotten around to autopsying him. So, perhaps he had never been dead at all.

And why couldn't anyone understand him? He longed to talk to Linda, to explain exactly what had happened and why he was on his way to her. If he hadn't gone to see Matt, he might have been able to blame poor cell phone service. Still, he had spoken to Matt in person and he couldn't understand a word he said. It all sounded perfectly normal to Paul, but others seemed unable to make out his words.

Then he hit on a brilliant idea. Without looking in the mirror, he took the next exit and steered the car toward a shopping center parking lot. He parked at the farthest side of it, away from everyone else. Then he pulled his cell phone out of his pocket.

His phone had digital voice recording applications, though he had never used them. Smiling, he turned on the radio and was greeted with nothing but static. With a frown, he moved to change stations but when his finger struck the SEEK button, to his horror, the fingernail flew off his index finger.

Eyes bulging, he stared at his finger, drawing it slowly closer to his eyes as he did so. The nail had flown completely off; not just part of the nail but all of it. There was no blood.

He recovered from this realization slowly, eyes snapping back to the radio as a religious station blared threats of hell at him. "You have no idea," he chuckled to himself.

Carefully, so as not to repeat the nail-loss incident, he started the voice recording. He let it run for a count of ten, and then stopped the recording. He lowered the volume and hit the playback on his phone. The regurgitated ramblings of some preacher or other assaulted his ears. Annoying, but exactly the same as he had heard it the first time.

Next, he hit the record button and cleared his throat. "Testing one, two, three. Testing, testing, and testing some more." He switched it off.

He took a moment to steel himself against what he might hear next, then shut his eyes and hit the playback.

"Aaaaarrrr! Garrrrg! Uh-uh-uh-uuuuuhhhhh!"

Paul dropped the phone and nearly screamed. That was what everyone else heard when he spoke? He placed one hand on his chest and shut his eyes, trying to gather enough courage that he could play the recording again, just to be sure.

The same. It was just the same. Paul started to cry but no tears would come. He wanted to slam his fist against the dashboard, but he was afraid his hand might fly off or something.

He began to yell, gesturing wildly as he mocked fate. "So that's it then? I stepped in some goo and then I may or may not have died. My penis doesn't work. Parts of me keep falling off. And people can't even understand me when I talk!"

Something outside the car window caught his sight and he looked over to see a middle-aged woman staring at him. It dawned on him then how it must have looked: Some crazy guy, sitting alone in the car, ranting and raving at no one in particular. He put the car back into gear and drove off before she could call the cops or something.

"What am I going to do?" he kept asking himself. "What in the hell am I going to do?"

He drove on toward California, sitting as still as possible lest he lose any more parts. He had another four hundred miles before he would need gas again and he intended to put that four hundred miles behind him as quickly as he could.

CHAPTER FOUR

Paul continued to make his way toward California, reasoning with himself all the way. He argued first that he couldn't have died because he hadn't soiled himself. Okay, so his penis didn't work but that could be explained away, too.

"Maybe I got some sort of infection," he mused. "That sounds reasonable. I got an infection and I can't pee. And maybe that infection is what's causing my hand to break and my fingernail to fall off. Sure! There's a perfectly logical explanation for all of this."

He chuckled but the sound, even to his ears, was offensive. The only good thing was that the police weren't after him. Apparently, his best friend….his best friend…

…Matt! His best friend's name was Matt. And Matt hadn't called the police on him.

How could he possibly forget his best friend's name?

His phone rang again, singing out with Linda's ring tone. It was about time to get gas again anyway, so he pulled off at the exit and slipped the car into another gas mall lot.

"Hello, baby," he said, certain that she wouldn't understand him, but wanting to try anyway.

"Aw, my poor baby!" she cooed. "Still not feeling any better? I'm so sorry." She paused for a moment, in the hopes that he could get some sort of message across, apparently. When he didn't even try, she pressed on. "I just called to see how you were feeling. No better, I hear. Well, you just rest and take your meds. I'll call again in the morning to check in on you. I love you, baby, and I hope you feel better soon."

"I love you, too, Linda. You have no idea." But all that came out was a series of groans and growls, he knew.

The call ended and Paul sat staring straight ahead. The sun had begun to set and this time it was the west's turn to put on a coat of many colors.

Someone knocked on the window so suddenly that Paul jumped and momentarily juggled the phone. "Hey buddy! You gonna gas that thing or what?" The guy bent low to peer in through the window, and then his face fell. The man suddenly paled, held out both hands, and backed away. "I'm so sorry. I didn't know. Sorry."

Paul watched as the man got into his car and peeled out. "What the hell—?" Paul looked in the visor mirror and hollered. There were blotches all over his face now and the left side of his lip had dropped to the point where several teeth showed through the gap. He choked back a scream and looked around frantically, trying to find some way of concealing his face. Several ideas—such as wearing an overly large hoody—occurred to him but every idea he had required him to get out of the car.

With no other avenue open to him, he got quickly out of the car and swiped his card. Several people seemed to notice him, but looked away of their own accord. For now, he would depend on the fact that most people would fear some kind of infection and would stay away from him. That would work for a while, or so he hoped.

There were several things he had to take care of while he was stopped, but he would have to wait for total darkness to get out of the car. A sudden pain gripped his stomach, doubling him over and radiating to his head where it settle in as a dull throb.

"Of course! I'm hungry." Paul laughed, a genuinely good-natured sound. "I can't even remember the last time I ate. Or slept. Christ! And no wonder I haven't peed. I haven't had anything to drink in days."

He almost pushed open the car door and got out, but thought better of it before his hand even hit the handle. He would get food and drink later. He had waited this long; a little longer wouldn't matter. Besides, there was something he had to do right now.

He pulled out his cell phone again and clicked in to his email. He addressed the email to Linda and began to type on the tiny keyboard:

My darling Linda:

No, this isn't what you think. LOL It's not a dear Linda letter. But I have something important to tell you and I wanted to tell you before I got there. Right now, I'm really on my way to you. The last two times you've called me, I was in the car, driving to you. From the moment I laid eyes on you, I've loved you with all my heart. I know we agreed that I wouldn't join you until my ten years with the city were up and I could quit and still get my pension. I know I have only two weeks left to go. But something happened at work the other day and it changed me forever. I can't talk about it right now and I won't bore you with it. But I had to come to you right away.

I hate to be cryptic about it all. Fact is, I might not make it there at all. Strike that. I WILL make it there if it kills me. I love you more than life itself and nothing on this earth is going to keep me from you. I'll be there in five days and I have something important to ask you when I get there. Please, don't ever lose faith in me.

All my love always,

Your Paul

He sat back and read over the email, wishing for all the world that he were some sort of poet. Linda was the English major and her words flowed like sweet nectar from a flower….

"Hey! That was downright poetic, wasn't it?" He chuckled then, and began to re-read the email.

He had no other choice. He had to let her know what was going on. Even though his own sin had been one of omission, he still felt like he was lying to her. He hated to lie to Linda. It caused him physical pain. Or, it would if he still felt pain.

The sun was nearly set. Paul clicked SEND and sat back against the seat. Again, his stomach roiled, though it really wasn't in just his stomach but sort of all through his torso. It doubled him over and made him groan, then a dull ache settled into his head and took up permanent residence.

Paul waited. He waited for the sun to set, he waited for the pain in his stomach and head to subside, and he waited for an answer from Linda. An hour later, the sun was completely down and he decided to make his way into the convenience store. The light blazed out through the glass front, illuminating a large portion of the parking lot in front but the eaves cast a long, thin shadow directly in front of the store. He kept to that shadow and tried to avoid other people whenever possible without seeming suspicious.

Is that the right term for me anymore? he wondered. *Am I really even human anymore? What am I? What's happened to me?*

He slipped in through the glass door and was greeted with the BING

BONG! of the door alarm. It startled him for a moment but he slipped behind the first row of shelves he saw, trying to avoid anyone's gaze without acting completely squirrelly. He grabbed a Ding Dong, a soda, one of the XXL hoodies that hung on a make-shift rack near the beer cooler. He would have to pay and when he did, he would have to face the guy at the counter.

He saw now that the guy at the counter was watching him, tracking his movements in the convex mirrors that littered the store's ceiling line. Paul straightened and tried to act a little less like a thief and more like a human being. There were no other customers in the store at the moment. That much was in his favor. Screwing up his confidence, he approached the counter, head down, and placed his items next to the register. Best to face it head-on.

"I apologize for my appearance," he muttered, not quite meeting the young man's gaze.

The young man looked confused at the garbled noises issuing from Paul's mouth, but he offered a smile anyway. To Paul's delight, the guy chuckled. "It's all right. I've seen worse. Every morning." The man dropped his own arm onto the counter with a hard thump. It was a muscular arm right down to the elbow, where it terminated in a mangled lump of flesh. "Explosion in Velusia."

"Fire," Paul offered, stabbing one finger in the direction of his face. "No money for skin grafts."

The man smiled and rang up Paul's purchases. He swiped Paul's card, proffered the receipt and placed the items in a bag. Just as Paul turned to leave, the man grasped his arm and pulled him around so as to catch his gaze. The man's eyes were piercing, commanding, and the most understanding that Paul had ever seen.

"Don't ever be ashamed. What you are on the outside doesn't determine what you are on the inside. Hold your head up, look people straight in the eye, and don't back down from life, you hear?"

Paul nodded and tried to smile around his droopy lip. "Thank you. So much."

He gathered the bag into his arms and walked toward the door, keeping his head up for as long as he was in the man's sight. Then he lowered his head and bolted for the car.

Convinced that he needed to eat, Paul unwrapped the Ding Dongs as he went, greedily stuffing one into his mouth and chewing frantically. He swallowed hard, felt the searing pain in his stomach, and bent over and puked. A loud "eeeew!" came from the kid hanging out of his mom's car window and Paul hurried along, wiping bits of snack cake from his chin.

Maybe it had just been too long since he last ate. Perhaps his system just wasn't ready for the shock of a pure jolt of sugar. Whatever the reason, Paul gave the soda a shot. He hadn't peed in days and he chalked it up to the fact that he hadn't drunk anything in days. He took a tentative sip, which went down cold and sweet. Then he took two more gulps and waited for the inevitable burp.

Instead, he vomited soda and the remaining bits of snack cake all over the outside of the car door. In abject misery, he began to sob then, his body shaking with the effort, soft mewling sounds issuing from his lopsided mouth. Still, no tears came.

He sat still for a few minutes, trying to regain his composure and letting his stomach calm down to a dull roar. There was still a wringing, aching sort of pain in his gut, as if someone were trying to squeeze the last bits of life from his unused parts. His head ached and, when he looked into the mirror, he noted with horror that there were more blotches than before and his lower lip had slipped even further down, giving him a menacing sort of grimace.

His mind settled on one immutable fact: He had to get to Linda before he completely fell apart. He started the engine and put the car in gear, resolved to reach her before she lost faith in him. He was deteriorating at an alarming rate and there was no time to waste.

The GPS barked its familiar "recalculating" message at him twice, and then gave him a direction in which to go. Back to the highway, merge, drive straight ahead for another 30 hours. The pain in his gut made itself known once more as he cruised along at a steady pace. He drove for another two hours without incident before his phone signaled an incoming email. He picked up his phone and glanced at the message.

Linda. She had answered his email. He would have to pull over for this one.

A rest stop loomed ahead and he took the exit slowly. It was one of those large affairs, with a mini mart attached and enough parking for hundreds of cars. Paul chose a space far from the buildings and away from the other vehicles. He pulled in and switched off his headlights, actually turning the car off and rolling down the window. He had learned through experience that hot or cold were both the same to him and that the stuffiness of the car with its windows closed seemed to affect him not at all.

He clicked on the email and watched tensely as it opened. There was a smiley after the signature. That was a good sign.

> *My dearest Paul:*
>
> *Whatever has happened, know that I love you with all my heart and I stand behind you no matter what. I'll be waiting here for you, aching to see you again, my love.*
> *Always,*
>
> *Your Linda*

Paul smiled, or what passed for a smile these days. She still loved him and trusted him enough not to interrogate him through email. God! What had he ever done to deserve such a wonderful woman? The thought of her was what kept him going, moving on toward something rather than simply praying for a real, permanent death. He knew that if he could just get to Linda, hold her, rest his head in her lap and hear the sound of her voice—then—then everything would be all right.

Another odd thought occurred to him: In all the time since this whole fiasco started, he hadn't once slept or even rested. Usually, it took four or five mugs of coffee to keep him moving through his day. Upon reflection, he found that he wasn't the least bit tired.

"How can I not be tired?" he said to himself softly.

Maybe he was tired and didn't know it. Maybe the adrenaline and fear had propelled him through the past two days. Whatever the cause, he felt sure that he would be better off if he just got a little rest.

He got out of the car then, stretching his legs even though they weren't stiff just because it seemed like the thing to do. Then, he climbed into the back seat and stretched out, laying one thin arm across his eyes to shut out the light streaming from the huge bulbs overhead.

After a few moments, he rolled onto his side, this being his usual position for good sleeping. To no avail, he rolled onto his back. He tried everything he knew: meditation, clearing his mind, counting backward from one hundred. A stone cold nerd to the core, he even tried factoring Fibonacci's numbers as far as he could. No power on earth would make him sleep.

He was about to abandon all hope and drive back to the freeway when someone jerked open the driver's side door and leapt into the car. Panic ripped through Paul's very core and he sat bolt upright in the back seat just as the man turned over the engine.

"What the hell are you doing?" Paul demanded in his new growly-voice.

The man spun around in his seat in one swift movement, staring daggers through Paul. "Just shut up and sit still and I won't hurt you."

Panic gave way to stark raving terror and then morphed into sheer madness. Paul's mind snapped. He felt it give way even as he lunged over the back of the seat, one hand locking into the man's hair and pulling his head to the side as his jaw opened impossibly wide. He drove his teeth into the man's neck with every ounce of force he had left in him.

CHAPTER FIVE

Linda had been puzzled by Paul's email. It sounded so ominous, so frighteningly vague that she had stared at it for a long time before answering. She had decided to be supportive in the end, if for no other reason than that she trusted Paul and he deserved that trust. But now, unanswered questions nagged at her and twisted her stomach into knots.

Paul was the most conscientious driver she had ever met. He had never even had a parking ticket and he would never, for any reason, text or talk on the phone while he was driving. She knew that he would pull off to the side of the road to read every email, answer every call. It would impede his progress if she kept bugging him. The only other person who might have the answers she sought was Matt, and she fully intended to have those answers.

She had to scroll down to find Matt's cell number. He wasn't exactly her favorite person. He was Paul's best friend and for that reason alone, he had made it onto her speed dial list. If Paul weren't in the picture, she wouldn't hang out with Matt, but she wouldn't snub him either. Matt was just sort of there, like a loyal spaniel or your stupid little brother. You had to love him. *Had* to.

It took four rings for Matt to utter his usual answer. "Say words."

"Matt? It's Linda." She heard the TV in the background go silent and she could picture Matt sitting up and trying to act like he was not stoned.

"Hey, Linda." He laughed nervously. "What's the haps?"

"I got a strange email from Paul a while ago. I was hoping you could help clarify it."

"Uh … shouldn't you ask Matt?" Now, he sounded really nervous, he knew. It went beyond pot paranoia.

"I don't want to bother him every few minutes. You know he pulls off the road every time he has a call."

"Sure." People had a way of making Matt tell them things he never wanted to say in the first place. Linda could almost hear the wheels in his head spinning as he worried over what to say. "So, what is it you want to know?"

"Paul said he's on the way here, to LA."

"Yea."

"And he said that something horrible happened at work." She paused, letting him mull that over. "What was it that happened, exactly?"

"Well…uh…I think maybe Paul should be the one to tell you."

"Did he get fired?"

"No."

"Did he quit?"

"No." Matt felt sweat break out on his brow. He swallowed hard.

"Did he get in a fight? Or get injured? Is he sick?"

"Not any of those, no. I can't tell you, Linda. I can't. It's Paul's place to tell you when he gets there. That's why he's coming. He just wants to see you…" He stopped right there, just shy of saying, "one last time."

"See me…why?" She wondered if Paul was going to break up with her. What if he was seeing someone else? What if he decided he didn't want to live in Los Angeles after all? "Is he breaking up with me?"

"No way." Matt wondered why women always went there first. Linda was not an insecure woman and Paul had never given her reason to doubt him or herself. And yet, her first assumption was that Paul had met someone else and so he was dumping her.

"Is he seeing somebody else? Did he change his mind about coming out here to live?" She thought she might cry. Her hands twisted at her shirt the same way her guts were twisting at her.

"Linda, honest to God. Paul loves you so much. And he's not ever gonna break up with you and he wouldn't cheat on you if somebody put a gun to his head. Why would he drive all the way to California to tell you he didn't want to come to California?"

"Then tell me what the hell's going on!" she snapped, tears filling the corners of her eyes. "Tell me before I go stark raving mad!"

"I'm sorry, Linda. I'm so sorry. I just can't. Paul will tell you when he gets there, but I can't tell you anything. Just trust me when I say that this is not entirely a bad thing. He'll fix everything…"

"Not 'entirely'? What's that supposed to mean?" She was screaming now and she knew it. But she just couldn't stop. Hysteria had taken over and she felt her brain melting with the heat of it, making her more frantic by the moment. "And what's he going to fix? Matt?"

Matt hung up. She knew he was avoiding her. He couldn't take the pressure of keeping Paul's secret and of lying to her, or the chance of letting anything slip out. So, he simply hung up. She called back almost immediately, but there was no answer. She called six more times in quick succession with the same result. Frustrated, she gave up, not sure if she was angry at Matt, angry at Paul, or just frightened.

What the hell am I doing?

With that thought fresh in his mind, Paul locked his teeth into the man's flesh, pulling back with his head and pushing away with his hands. The man screamed; his hands flailed madly about as he sought escape.

Paul heard flesh tear, felt the hot rush of blood as it spurted out of the man's body and into his own. Then, he was leaning back, chewing, swallowing, devouring that hunk of torn-away flesh. A sense of relief washed over him as he swallowed.

The man's screams ended in a soft, wet gurgle as he died, and Paul leaned forward to rip another strip of meat from the guy's shoulder, than another from his neck. He was drenched in blood now but as he ate, the pain in his head and gut subsided. The taste was not unpleasant, the texture not nearly as disturbing as he might have thought.

Half the man's neck and shoulder were gone now. *Over the teeth and past the gums,* Paul thought, leaning back. He swallowed that last mouthful and licked his lips. A sort of peace came over him for a moment, his screaming gut finally quiet and his mind clear. He felt stronger somehow, more alive.

Then his eyes fell on the man with the gaping neck and he began to scream. He screamed and screamed, his mind ripping apart at the thought of what he had just done. The smell of blood had filled the air and, had he been able to smell properly, it would have made him vomit. Indeed, he tried to make himself vomit, to give up those chunks of human flesh which he had greedily ripped from the man.

Stricken, he looked crazily about for signs that anyone had heard his screams, had seen what happened. There didn't seem to be anyone else around, so maybe he'd gotten away with it. He wasn't even sure he wanted to get away with it. That one act had sent him careening over a line that no one but a monster would cross.

Was that what he was now? A monster? Had he no humanity left in him?

He thought for a moment. He had just committed a heinous act, had been in real danger of being found out. He should be scared—terrified, in fact—his heart racing, his lungs heaving for air. He put his hand over his heart and felt no tell-tale pounding. There was no rapid rise and fall of his chest.

In desperation, he placed his finger over his wrist, his neck, everywhere he could think of to find a pulse that just wasn't there. His heart didn't beat; he didn't breathe.

"Oh my God," he muttered, his gaze falling on the dead body before him. "I'm dead. Not dead…undead. I'm an undead, flesh-eating zombie monster!"

He rested his head on the window and began to weep. There were still no tears but his body, wracked with sobs, convulsed against the door. He didn't know what to do next. How could he get rid of the body? Should he even keep driving? Surely, he couldn't present Linda with a ring and an undead zombie parody of himself. Everything had changed and he didn't know how to adjust.

Very suddenly, he felt like everything he had tried to do was just an exercise in futility. Linda certainly couldn't love him this way. He wasn't even sure he wanted her to. He wasn't sure he wanted to live. Not that he was really alive…

He shook his head to clear it. How to get rid of the body? Maybe the best thing now was just to drive straight to the nearest police station and turn himself in for the undead flesh-eater he was. They couldn't possibly blame him. After all, he hadn't done this to himself. And since becoming a monster hadn't been his doing, they couldn't possibly blame him for eating, for trying to survive. Could they?

He thought to himself that none of this had been his doing and that he had no other choice but to survive. He had to survive and get to Linda. Even if she didn't want him, he had to give her the option. The dead guy in the front seat had tried to rob him—he had defended himself.

With his mind made up to keep driving toward Linda at all costs, he slipped into the passenger side of the front seat. He would conceal the body until he reached Linda, then base all further decisions on her reaction to the situation. Yes, that was it! He would let Linda decide it all. All he had to do was get to her.

He hefted the body over the back of the seat and let it drop onto the floor of the car with a sickening thud. The trunk's floor cover was removable and so he pushed the button that unlocked the trunk latch. As quickly as he could, he retrieved the floor cover and threw it over the dead hunk of meat in the back seat. Satisfied that he had done the best job he could of concealing the body, he climbed back into the driver's seat…and that's when he saw it.

He caught a glimpse of himself in the rear view mirror as he slid into the seat. Leaning forward, he stared into a face that was free from those black and green blotches. His lips were full and even again, his eyes even seemed brighter. His heart still didn't beat and he wasn't breathing, but he looked more like a living human again.

Paul tried on a smile, less rictus-like and more endearing now. Slowly, he nodded to himself and chuckled.

"So that's it! I eat live flesh and I become more alive."

A sudden fascinating thought occurred to him just then: If he had eaten a little flesh and had become more alive, more whole, would it not follow that eating *more* flesh would make him more alive?

He felt like a scientist, studying some weird biological phenomena, at least that's what he told himself so that he could climb into the back seat and eat more of the bastard who had tried to steal his car. He ate most of the man's right hand and forearm, and then felt for a pulse. Nothing.

Disappointed, he consoled himself with the fact that at least he appeared more normal now, if more than a little blood spattered, and he felt stronger. He started the car and backed out of the space. As long as no one found the body in his back seat, he would be fine. The man had been less than a stellar example of humanity, so maybe he had done the world a service. Maybe he had even saved a life, killing the bastard before he could kill someone else. And that is how Paul Tremblay, son of Marge and Joe Tremblay, soon-to-be fiancé of Linda and best friend of Matt managed to cope with his current condition. Zombie-ism had been forced upon him and, with that new state of being, had come the ability to prevent crime and save lives by eating from the lower belly of society. Amen!

CHAPTER SIX

It wasn't until the warning light came on and the beep sounded that Paul realized he had a real problem. He was almost out of gas and in his current state—covered with blood and smelling of death—he would have a hard time getting the gas he needed. People might be able to dismiss a bit of black-and-green blotchiness, but they sure weren't going to understand a cannibalistic murder.

The upcoming exit sported several gas stations, both large and small. Paul took the exit with the idea of dealing with his problems one at a time. First, he would clean himself up as much as possible, and then he would get his gas. He chose a small, independent station that looked as though it would have fewer customers at that hour.

He eased into the lot, parking in the shadows at first in order to assess his condition. Since eating a bit, he felt sharper, more able to deal with things than he had over the past few hours. Though the light was bad, one look in the rear view told him that he needed a shower. He might be able to remove his hoodie and eliminate that whole mess, but his face and hands were stained red with blood—and other things—and he needed a wash.

Paul and Matt had a favorite place to eat lunch. It was a little barbecue truck that generally parked off the intersection of 41st and 3rd. A wipe came with every meal and, since they always cleaned up in the station bathroom afterward, they tossed the wipes into the glove box for future use. To that end, Paul rooted around blindly, finally laying his hands on a cluster of them, secreted behind the breath mints and under the registration. He grabbed three and tore them open, using the dim light and the rear view to clean the blood and guts from his face.

Once he was satisfied that he was as presentable as a flesh-eater could be, he tossed the wipes into the back seat, threw the hoodie on top of them, and started the car again. He pulled up at the far side of the pumps and shut down the engine, then climbed out to fill the car.

No one was about at that hour, though the attendant inside gave him a cursory glance. With his hair all slicked back and his face freshly scrubbed, Paul looked respectable enough not to warrant a second look. He managed to fill the tank without interference and guide the car back to the highway.

He had gone perhaps ten miles when the phone rang. The sound of it scared him and the car lurched as he started. Then he picked the phone up and grimaced at it. It shone brightly, announcing the name of the caller. Matt.

"Who the hell is Matt?" he asked himself. "Matt." He frowned heavily and shook his head. "Matt."

No matter how many times he repeated it, the name meant nothing. There was Linda. His parents. But Matt? Try as he might, he could find no memory associated with Matt.

On a whim, he flipped through his contacts, finally landing on Matt's name. It showed his phone number—which he didn't recognize—and his address—which matched his own. "Ah, Matt!" he sighed with a smile.

How could he forget his best friend and roommate? He'd only known the guy for his entire life! And now he couldn't even remember who he was without prompting?

Paul clicked the green button on the screen and answered the phone. "Matt?"

"Oh good! You're still alive." Matt chuckled a bit and pressed on. "Listen, I know you can't talk…at least I can't understand you when you talk… but that's okay. I just wanted to say I'm sorry if I was too rough on you earlier. I know how important Linda is to you. And I want you to know I didn't call the police or anything. Just take care of the car, you know? We still owe on it and I would kind of like to keep it nice at least until we pay it off."

Paul thought of the torn-out trunk carpet, the dead body in the back seat, and the blood covering most of the interior. "OK," he said, forming the words as carefully as he could.

"Cool. Okay. I just wanted you to know we were cool and all. You take care, ok? And if you need anything…like…well…anything at all…you let me know."

The call ended and Paul frowned. "Sure, buddy," he chuckled to himself. "I'll take care. And I could use some help. Could you get the dead guy out of the back seat and maybe find a way to make me be NOT undead? As in, alive? As in, not eating people anymore? 'k, thanx bye!"

* * *

Paul had been driving straight ahead for two hours. Blessedly, he didn't require sleep, food (at least not beyond the occasional taste of the corpse back there) and he didn't need to stop to relieve himself. He made good time.

Most of the time, his eyes were fixed, unblinking, on the windshield. His mind was a complete blank. It wasn't that he had repressed any of the last two days, but that his mind quite simply would not contain thought unless it was forced. It seemed like years since he had left New York; years more until he would reach LA.

"Keep left!" the electronic voice boomed at him through the silence.

Paul cried out and for a heart-stopping moment, he thought that the dead guy who had lain on the floor for the last 300 miles had somehow been revived; that somehow, he, Paul, had turned the poor bastard into a zombie.

Then his eyes flashed to the dash and realized that the GPS was the owner of that voice, as cold and dead as the guy in the back seat. He did what the GPS advised. He kept right. But for the life of him, he couldn't remember why. Where was he going again? Why was he going there?

He tried to force himself to remember. It was getting harder to recall things now, even simple things like his friends' names and how to check his email. He knew that one bite of his human snack-pack would fix it. But he had made himself a promise some time ago, and that was to never again taste of human flesh. He was saving the corpse for that one all-important moment when his pseudo-self was face-to-face with . . . with . . .

He began to cry then. Still no tears, but his body bucked and shook and he made a pitiable noise. He was on his way to somewhere, to see his girlfriend, whose name he couldn't remember. He made a mental note and hoped that it would stick: When he next needed gas, he would check his phone and remember her name. Then he would write it on one of the sticky notes that . . . that . . . what's his name . . . always kept in the car for leaving messages on people's doors.

Paul drove on. The fact that this had happened at all was distressing enough but coupled with the fact that he was forgetting simple things drove him almost over the brink. Why had this happened to him? He was a good person. He was smart. He did favors for his friends without being asked. He never once called in sick to work when he wasn't sick. And while those other city-fed fat-cats relied on the fact that they couldn't get fired and wasted the day smoking and shooting the breeze, he carried out his duties faithfully. He'd had a plan from the time he was sixteen; he knew how his life should go. He had never once deviated from that plan; had worked arduously toward its completion. And now, a mere two weeks from the realization of his life's dreams, *this* had happened.

His mind blanked again. He took a curve in the highway too fast, made the body in the back seat shift, and scared himself. He checked the mirror and noticed that several blotches had broken out on his face. One check of his hands revealed even more.

"I won't do it," he snapped to no one but himself. "I won't eat human flesh again. I don't care how bad it gets, I won't do it."

And with that total conviction set firmly in his mind, he drove on.

A huge power line joined up with the road and followed it for a while. It stayed with him for nearly twenty miles, then branched off and disappeared. Paul's phone rang and he snatched at it, looking at the name on the screen.

Linda.

And the battery was at twenty-one percent.

"Hello?" he barked.

There was a moment of silence and then, "I know you can't talk. Where are you? Are you almost here?"

Did she even know how far it was from New York to LA? "I've got a long way to go, baby. I'm driving as fast as I can."

Linda sighed. "Email me when you can. Let me know where you are. If you're going to arrive during the day, I'll stay home from work. But I need to know when you'll be here." There was a pause. It cut like a dagger. "Bye, Paul."

Linda. Paul dropped the phone onto the seat and groaned. "No, I love you? No, I can't wait to see you, Paul? No, I miss you?"

It became painfully obvious to him then that she was losing interest in him. He had pissed her off, made her doubt him with all this craziness. He had to get to her. Fast.

If only he had taken a plane. Why hadn't he taken a plane?

The gas warning bleeped at him again and he trained his eyes on the signs ahead. There was a SuperMart at the next exit. He would pull off there and get some gas. It was going to be tricky, though. The sun was up and he knew his car was a mess. The mirror taunted him; told him that he was a mess, too.

He eased onto the exit ramp, watching the road ahead for signs of the SuperMart. There were signs everywhere, though, and he had trouble finding the one he needed. Then fate stepped in and guided him in the guise of a giant sign that blared red against blue, SuperMart.

The parking lot was huge. Morning commuters were pulling in and out, getting their coffee, their donuts, their energy drinks. Cars moved so quickly through the process that it was almost like watching a time-lapse video.

There was parking all around the building. The door opened into the front of it, the delivery and service door opened into the right. Paul pulled toward the left side of the building, the only one with no doors and no glass. He maneuvered the car until he could back into the space, putting the bloody driver's side on the wooded edge of the lot. He needed to gas up, but first he had some cleaning up to do. If he tried to just pull up to the pumps, someone would see all that blood and he would be done for.

Once he had stepped from the car, his mind felt clearer. He pulled his hair forward, so that it covered his eyes and the edge of his face, trying for that fine line between armed robber and gangsta. His plan was to go into the SuperMart, grab an energy drink and a donut (which he would throw away) and a bottle of window cleaner and some papers towels (which he would use to clean the blood off the car). He had this all mapped out in his head, repeating it to himself as he walked, trying not to let those precious plans slip away from him in a moment of thoughtlessness.

It was a good plan, as plans went. It came very close to working, too.

Paul bent his head low and slipped into the store, making sure to face away from the camera aimed at the door. He slid to the back of the store where the coolers were, grabbed himself a small energy drink, then paced over two aisles to pick up a bag of donuts. It was easier and quicker, he reasoned, to grab a bag than to fuss with the rack that held the single donuts. Cleaning products were to the right, paper products to the left. He grabbed the window cleaner first, then made for the paper products.

His hands full now, he marched to the checkout and placed the items on the counter. At the far end of the counter was a rack of hoodies, fifty percent off. He grabbed an XXL and tossed it on the counter with his other items. He kept his head down and coughed every now and again. If the clerk thought he was really sick, he would be more likely to hurry him through the process. Paul dug around in his pocket, produced a twenty, then scooped up his items and headed for the door.

The cool morning air hit him as he stepped outside, clutching the bag to his chest and making sure not to make eye contact with anyone. Briefly, he stopped on the sidewalk, pulling the hoodie out of the bag and over his head. He strode purposefully down the sidewalk and rounded the corner . . .

There were two cops and a cruiser sitting on that side of the parking lot. Paul felt instant panic well up inside of him and he ducked back around the corner. He wondered what had tipped them off. Even knowing the blood was there, he couldn't see it from where he stood. How did they see it?

He managed to peek around the corner again. No sir! They weren't leaving any time soon. If Paul had had a heartbeat, he was sure it would be pounding right now. His phone was in the car. The GPS that knew where he was going was in the car. He needed that car!

There were only two choices, he knew. One, he could look for a car that had been left running, slip into it and hope that he could drive casually out of the lot before the owner saw him. He looked around. All the cars seemed to be either occupied or shut up and locked. He could stand there and wait for one of the drivers to get out and leave their car but every second he stood there, he risked being found out.

And that brought him to choice number two. He could run. Running, the international sign of guilt. But how far could he get if he just nonchalantly walked away? Twenty yards? Maybe fifty?

There was no other recourse left to him. He had to get away from the SuperMart without the cops—or anybody else—seeing him do it. Quickly, he dumped the tell-tale bag into the trash, turned on his heels, and walked away from the place. And as he turned, the lead policeman came around the corner. He turned that corner just in time to see Paul's back walking away.

CHAPTER SEVEN

This town was a small town, suffering from all the same pains that other small towns suffered. Its death or growth rested on the shoulders of its industry. At present, this town's industry was farming and it was thriving, thank you very much. The nearby river and rich soil that surrounded it meant that crops flourished. Calm winters, moist summers, and an employee pool of thousands meant that a farmer would have to be awfully stupid to fail.

And like most small towns in their prepubescent years, this one suffered from a sort of reverse big bang. Its center had started to die, the old original buildings marked with decay, the crime following the decay like a flock of vultures. And as the center died, the town grew from the inside out. New businesses chose prime locations on the outskirts of town. Old businesses relocated to the higher-traffic, newer parts of the town, each according to their stability and ability. The further out into the country you got, to a point, the richer and grander the homes were. If you were a CEO or a doctor, you lived in one of those neatly planned and carefully staged subdivisions. Old school lived on the hill. And if you were the single mom welfare recipient, you lived at the center of town, where grand old houses had been turned into festering eyesores.

The growth, death and re-growth of the town, if seen from space in a time-lapsed video, would look like the blooming of a flower. What would appear in that video in a matter of seconds had taken over a hundred years, but it had happened nonetheless. People, whether happy about the way things were going or not, all had opinions, and those opinions kept them separate from one another, kept them struggling.

Paul didn't know anything about the little town into which he had escaped. He didn't even know its name. All Paul knew was that he had to get his stuff out of his car, and that the police had the car. By now, they knew who it was they were looking for. Paul only knew two things: First, that he was on his way to LA to find Linda, and that he could not let the police catch him before he did.

He walked away from the SuperMart, keeping to the shadows and small backstreets of the little town. Whenever possible, he cut through alleys and skulked behind houses. All he wanted to do at that point was to get to some place, any place, where he felt safe. But safe was a relative term.

He was a murderer now and the whole world knew it. How long it would take before the police contacted Matt and Linda, he had no idea, but very soon, Linda would think him a monster. Was there really any point in carrying on with this silly plan? Wasn't it better to just turn himself in, try to explain, and take his licks? Surely they would eventually come to see that all of it had been beyond his control. He was no longer human in any way that mattered and so could not be blamed for what he had done. No, he couldn't have Linda thinking that the love of her life was a killer. He had to get to her and tell her his side.

And so Paul developed his Mantra. Things were slipping from his mind so quickly that he could barely carry a sentence from beginning to end without forgetting it. And so he marched on through the town, chanting.

I have to get to Linda in LA. I have to get to Linda in LA.

He considered himself the luckiest duck in town, since he had managed to travel that far without being seen. Surely, the cops had put out an APB on him already. How long could it take for them to peruse his phone and find his name, address, every single bit of personal information there was to know about him?

At that thin line which divided the industrial outskirts of town from the inner-town slums, Paul found an old and long-forgotten club. It harkened back to the days when the good folks of the town hadn't so much minded having a "gentleman's club" around and when the back of said club was operated by the local madam. The neon sign was all but gone. Only the high-kicking legs of the animated stripper remained. The door was chained, though that chain looked like it had been strained to its limits on more than one occasion.

A layer of grime coated the door handle as Paul put his hand on it. The handle itself was warm from the sunshine that bathed it. He gave it a pull and the door opened a good eighteen inches. Paul ducked down and slipped under the chain and through the opening. He was saved.

All was darkness inside. The plywood that had been studiously nailed over the window blocked out any form of light that might have penetrated glass. There was no electricity anymore, so none of the lights would work, even if the bulbs had managed to survive all those years. Paul tried to get his eyes to adjust to the darkness, but it was complete. There was not a bit of light to see by. He was blind.

He felt his way slowly across the room. If he barked one foot or banged one shin, he might well lose that part of himself forever. It was something that he didn't want to think about.

He found his way across the room and to the bar. By now, his hand was well and goodly coated with a film of dust. Everything had dust on it in there and he was sure that if he had some light, he would see that the air was thick with the dust he'd stirred up just by moving slowly through the room.

His hands traveled the length of the bar, first on top, then on the first shelf and then the second. He was looking for anything he might use to create light. A flashlight. Matches. A barbecue lighter. Anything.

He knocked a glass to the floor and it shattered. He winced from the sound and stood still for a moment, waiting to see if there was anybody else in there who might come running at the sound. When no one did, he began his search anew, hoping that luck would hang out with him for just a little longer.

His hands closed on something big and rectangular. It felt like cardboard but the humidity and dust gave it kind of a spongy feel. He pulled it off the bottom shelf and ran his fingers carefully over it, feeling as they rounded the long side and rubbed on something that felt like sandpaper.

Matches. He had found a big box of matches. No doubt, some bartender in years past had used them to make flaming drinks. Now, they were Paul's Godsend.

He opened the box carefully so as not to spill the contents, which rattled around the box as if they had a life of their own. He removed a match and closed the box, hoping against hope that the humidity hadn't destroyed any chance he had of lighting it.

He placed his hands just so, being careful. When he finally had worked up the nerve to try, he dragged the end of the matchstick along the sandpapered side and almost cheered with joy when it lit.

The room around him was cast into a tight circle of light. He could see the bar, the stools, a few of the tables that scattered across the floor like drunken dancers. What he needed now was the office. He wanted to find a pen and some paper. First he would write down all the things he had to remember, like Linda's name, her address, Matt's phone number, where he was headed. Then, he would write a letter to the people he cared about to serve as a last will and testament should he finally expire.

Expire.

Like rotted meat. That's all he was now, wasn't it? Rotted meat that, for some reason, was still able to ambulate.

He moved off toward the little hallway to his left, hoping that was the way to the office. If he could just find pen and paper, all his problems would be solved.

Linda slid in the door and dropped her purse and keys on the table in the little space she liked to call the foyer. It was in no way a real foyer, just a bit of tile floor adrift in the sea of carpet. She turned the latch on the door and took a quick peek in the mirror over the table. She was looking haggard, she knew. Perhaps she should invest a little money and go to the salon before Paul arrived. They hadn't seen each other in a while. What if he found her less desirable than he remembered?

With a heavy sigh, she wandered into the kitchen and opened the fridge door. There were two containers of left-over takeout food in there: One definitely gone, one questionable at best. She shut the door.

The day had been long and hard and she was so glad to be off work. But there was nothing in the apartment to eat, nothing worth doing. She snagged her phone from her purse and dialed the closest pizza joint, ordered a small pepperoni, then clicked through to her email. She had sent Paul an email at lunch time, reminding him that she needed to know where he was, when he would arrive. There was still no answer.

Wandering to the sofa, she dropped onto it with a soft Oof! She tossed the phone onto the sofa cushion and hugged her legs then, resting her chin on her knees. It wasn't like Paul not to answer her emails. She could understand him not wanting to talk on the phone, what with his being sick and all. But to not answer emails? That was so *not* Paul.

She hadn't liked Paul when she first met him. He had been a tad too shy, too unsure of himself and nervous. She generally liked a guy with more hutzpah. The more dominant males were definitely her type. But he had persisted and she had acquiesced, if only to get rid of him. He had asked her out the very first time they met, but she had shut him down. Then, he had had the gall to send her one red rose every hour until she agreed to go out with him. In the end, they had gone to Jeeters and she had a cool six dozen red roses in her apartment. Paul was persistent.

The memory of it all made her smile, then giggle. Her green eyes spar-kled and danced when she laughed. She knew that because Paul had said so about a hundred times.

Paul was a good man. He was thoughtful, neat, hard-working, loving, romantic, funny, smart, and loyal. Paul never broke promises and he never did anything to hurt anyone if he could help it. More than anything, she loved that one thing. They had never even had a fight.

She needed to touch up her roots, she remembered. She had let them go too long. Paul didn't care, of course. But she did.

By their second date, Linda had realized that Paul was THE ONE. He was MR. RIGHT, MR. PERFECT, HER BETTER HALF, HER SOUL MATE. By their fifth date, they were deciding their futures together; plan-ning just how their lives together would be.

"Dammit!" she spat and snatched the phone off the cushion. She dialed Paul's number and listened to it ring and ring, her smile running away from her. Then the voice mail kicked in and she sighed. "Hi, baby. I know you can't call. But I sent two emails and in case they didn't go through, I need to know you're okay. I need to know when you'll arrive so I can be here. Anyway . . . email me back. Or call and tap on the phone or some-thing. Anything. Just let me know you're okay. Love you. Bye."

Shutting off the phone, she dropped her feet to the floor and sank deeper into the sofa cushions. He wasn't ignoring her. He would never do that. Something was wrong, she just knew it. And she wasn't going to feel right until she knew that Paul was okay.

Paul sat behind the dust-coated desk of the former club owner, the pencil hovering over the paper as if waiting for permission to write. He had found a flashlight in one of the desk drawers and miracle of miracles, the thing had still worked. That pink bunny sure didn't lie.

Finally, he plunged ahead. He made note of Linda's full name, her phone number at the apartment and her cell phone number. Then, he wrote down her address (that one took a lot more thought) and made a small note below that so that he would remember where she worked. He continued writing, jotting down Matt's name and number, their shared address, and the license plate number of their car, should he ever need it.

All of this took him over an hour and he still wasn't sure that he had remembered all the details correctly. For example, the last four digits of

Linda's phone number might have been 0323 or 0232. He wasn't completely sure. Then he set about writing a farewell note to his loved ones. He began to cry halfway through, thinking of all that had happened to him, all that he'd done, and all the things he would never get to do again. When he was done, he sat back in the filthy chair and sighed. After staring at the paper for a long time, he folded it carefully and put it into his pocket.

He had no idea where to go from here. He couldn't just waltz into the police department and demand his car back. He was wanted for murder, after all. Aside from that, he looked like an extra from a Michael Jackson video.

The only thing to do was press on. He had to find another phone and another car. His face was severely blotched now and his stomach had begun to roil and cramp.

"You're not a thief," he said to the dark. "No, I'm broke."

CHAPTER EIGHT

Matt was kicked back on the couch, sucking down his third Pepsi and munching a bag of chips. In the ashtray next to him sat two roaches. The apartment smelled of pot and day-old pizza. On the TV: Some stupid show about Vikings. Matt didn't really like Vikings. He was just too lazy to reach for the remote.

There was a vicious knocking at his door then and it jolted him off the couch, making him spill his chips and nearly spill his Pepsi. He forced himself to sit up, though slowly, and he dumped the two roaches under the sofa.

"Damn," he muttered to himself, then, louder, "Coming! I'm coming!"

His large feet shuffled across the worn carpet as Matt made his way to the door. The chain was on, the lock was on. He stared at them for a few seconds while he decided which on the best procedure for opening the door. Finally, he unbolted the locks and opened it a few inches, peering out with one heavily-lidded eye.

"Detective Thomas Milligan of the NYPD." A badge shone through the crack in the door. "Are you Matt Cassidy?"

"Shit," Matt growled between clenched teeth. He cleared his throat, rubbed his face. "Yea, that's me. Matt Cassidy." Blink.

"Would you mind opening the door, sir? I'd like to have a word with you."

Matt pushed the door closed, ran a reckless hand through his hair and disengaged the chain. When he pulled the door open again, he was smiling. "How can I help you, officer?"

Clearly, the detective planned to come inside, but Matt managed to edge out the door and pull it shut behind him.

"You have a roommate? Paul Tremblay?"

The detective's eyes were piercing and Matt found himself shying away from them. "Yea, Paul and I live together. Why? What's wrong with Paul?"

"You own a car together? A brand new Toyota Camry, license number YKR 3182?"

"I don't know the license number, man, but yea. That's our car. And again I ask . . . what happened?"

"Your car was found parked outside a SuperMart in Lebanon, Kansas. It was covered in blood and there was a body in the back seat."

"Body?" Matt's chin dropped, his voice became deeper, more serious.

"The body of a man. We're not sure of his identity yet. He's still in the autopsy room. But the thing is, this guy was partially . . . eaten." The detective's eyes met Matt's and narrowed.

"Eaten?" Matt asked, as if he hadn't heard correctly. What in the hell did Paul do, he wondered? I don't want to get Paul into trouble, but I'm not going down for murder.

"Mr. Cassidy, where have you been for the last thirty-six hours? If I may ask."

"I went to work yesterday. There's like ten guys who can put me on the job. And this morning I got up around ten, and then I went to the bank to cash my check. Then I went to . . ." he stopped for a moment, thinking.

"Sir, when was the last time you saw your car?"

Matt stared at the detective, trying to figure a way out of all this without getting him and Paul in trouble. "Umm . . . the car was here three nights ago when I drove home from work in it. Look, detective, dude, I didn't kill nobody."

"I'm not saying you did, sir. But tell me, how did your car get all the way to Kansas and why was there a dead guy in the back seat?"

"I dunno, Mister." Matt collapsed against the door frame with a heavy sigh. "Listen, here's the thing: My roommate, Paul, he took the car three nights ago so he could go see his girlfriend." That was the honest to God truth, Matt realized, and he pressed on. "I haven't seen the car, or Paul, since then."

"This girlfriend, would that be Linda Gilchrist? Lives in Los Angeles?" Detective Milligan was reading from his little notebook. He looked up then to check Matt's face.

"Yea," Matt answered slowly.

"You should know," Milligan began, "that your friend, Paul's, fingerprints were all over the car. He was covered in blood and, my guess is, when the test results come back, we'll find that the blood is that of the deceased. We found Paul's phone in the car, but we haven't found Paul yet.

I'm working with the Lebanon police department on this, since our main suspect is a New York resident. So, if your buddy shows up or happens to call you, you tell him that he needs to come turn himself in. And then you call me. Here's my card." He flipped the card out with a flourish, as though he had done so a thousand times.

Matt suddenly realized that his jaw was hanging and he hadn't blinked in about five minutes. He let the gritty surface of his lids scrape over his dry eyes and swallowed. He took the card and tucked it into his pocket, his gaze never leaving Milligan's face.

Milligan turned and left then, without saying a word. Matt watched him go for a moment, then let himself slide down the door until he was sitting on the floor.

"Christ!" he groaned. "Paul, what have you done?"

Paul sat, curled up in the corner of the sofa, hugging his knees and rocking. Long periods lapsed during which he couldn't remember where he was, how he had gotten there, or what it was that he was supposed to do. All he knew was that it was very important that he do this thing.

He might have sat there forever, rocking and wondering, had the rat not come along. There were countless rats in the building; they pretty much ran the place. But Paul had been hearing this particular rat for the better part of an hour as it scurried along the shelves and rooted through a pile of debris on the floor next to the potted (dead) plant. Now, however, the rat had become emboldened and had made a bid for the sofa.

The creature managed to scratch and claw its way up the short arm of the sofa farthest from where Paul sat. It was perched on the sofa back now, glaring at him with beady eyes and cleaning its whiskers. Paul watched it without fear. Once you were (un)dead, what had you left to fear?

Then the rat ran along the back of the sofa, charging straight at Paul. Its intent was unclear but Paul, having worked the sewers for nearly ten years, had a natural aversion to rats. The minute the thing was in his reach, he lashed out with one hand. His original plan was to slap the thing away, make sure it didn't get to his face. But at the last second, his hand swiveled and he grabbed it tightly in his fist.

The rat squirmed for a moment, obviously stunned at its capture. Paul felt the whiskers working against his hand, sensed the creature's fear as he brought it closer to his face. And then the rat, in a final bid for freedom, bit him.

What followed then was the most disgusting and digestively horrid thing Paul had ever experienced. The rat, having filled its mouth with a good chunk of Paul, spat and squirmed and tried to get the taste of him out of its mouth. The feel of its little claws on Paul's hand drove him into revulsive rage and with a movement that was so quick and so unpremeditated that he couldn't have stopped himself if he'd tried, Paul popped the rat into his mouth.

There was a sickening snap and squish sound as Paul bit down on the rat. Blood filled his mouth and he found within a moment that the taste was not unlike the taste of the car-jacker. Paul chewed once, twice, swallowed the thing's head. And then he smiled.

The effect was almost instantaneous. At once, Paul's mind cleared, his memories began to return. He felt renewed strength and vigor. And if he'd had enough light and a clean enough mirror, he was certain that he'd find his face devoid of those ruptures and pustules. He smiled again.

It was all so clear to him now. He needed a new car . . . something nondescript but drivable. He also needed a map or a GPS or some other method of finding Linda. And he needed a source of food . . . or what passed as food for him these days.

Paul knew from experience that if you stole a car in the city, the reaction was immediate. The alarm went off, the police were called, an APB issued within the hour. Even in the absence of an alarm, most people would discover their car gone within two hours' time. But if you stole a car in the middle of the night, out in the country, it might go unnoticed for hours, even days. The odds were better if you stole someone's second car or a beater. If they didn't use it every day, they might not notice it was gone for a week or more. And out in the country, the cops took longer to get to the scene of the crime.

That was it then. Paul had to go out into the country and steal a car, perhaps an old farm truck or something. It might be morning before the cops arrived and the warrant was issued. But it had to be at night.

He focused his eyes on the plywood that covered the windows. There was a gap, albeit tiny, at the bottom left corner and light shone through. He would have plenty of time to gather his supplies and head out of town once the sun set.

He opened the drawers in the desk once more, finding the pen he had used before. He studied each object in the drawers, trying them on for size, hoping to find something else of use. At the back of the left top drawer, he found a stack of sticky notes—ah, sticky notes, my old friend—and he stuffed those, along with the pen, into his pocket. He found a pocket knife in the bottom right drawer and he took that too. His first car had been a beater and, when he couldn't afford to fix the dead starter, he had simply bypassed it and hotwired the thing, using the connection and disconnection of the wires as a form of starter. He would need the knife to cut and strip the wires.

Paul was not by nature a thief but his back was against the wall. He was wanted for a murder he couldn't really be faulted for being undead and, desperate. He wasn't sure how this all would end, but he made a mental note to return to this town if it all ended well, and pay back the guy for his car.

Paul fumbled his way to the front door, inching it open and looking outside for just a second. Judging by the position of the sun, he had a few hours before he would be able to leave. That in mind, he set about trapping another rat. He didn't like the idea, but if he was going to travel all the way out to the farm land on foot, he would need some sustenance.

Behind the bar was a small kitchen and it was in that direction that he heard the scuttling sounds of tiny rat feet as they searched for food, tended their young, whatever it was that rats did when left to their own devices. He felt his way to the kitchen and went in, planted himself in the middle of the floor and waited. He sat cross-legged for a little over an hour before a rat finally worked up enough courage to come close to him. When it did, Paul lashed out his hand and grabbed the thing, thrusting it under a large pot on the counter. He would keep it there until right before he left and then he would eat it.

Linda woke early that morning from a dream that scared the hell out of her. In this dream, Paul was falling out of the sky and she had been charged with catching him. But she had been given nothing more than a coffee cup to catch him in. She watched and waited as the small dot that was Paul fell through the air, trying to adjust her position so that she was always directly beneath him. Eyes turned skyward, she watched as the dot grew and became a man, fell faster. She aimed the cup, crying, and tried to figure out how in the world she was going to catch him in such a tiny vessel. All of a sudden, Paul simply melted, turning into a falling, trailing blob of goo which dropped into the cup, splattering Linda's shirt and making her scream.

She was still screaming when she woke up, her face and chest drenched in sweat and her entire body shaking. She threw back the covers and grabbed for her cell. There were no messages and no emails from Paul. Linda started to cry.

They had always been so close, so connected. Dreams aside, she knew him well enough to know when something was wrong. She hadn't heard from him for days and, even if he was still sick, that was unusual.

She had never wanted to be one of those stalker-chicks, checking up on her boyfriend every two hours, tracking him by the GPS, and whatnot. But she was scared now. She had called four times, sent five emails, and there had been not one answer. He could be dead, lying in a ditch somewhere, or at the bottom of a ravine, surrounded by smashed car parts.

Somewhere on that phone, she had Matt's number. Nobody had picked up at the apartment when she had called last night, so she tried to find Matt's cell number. He would know what was going on. He would put her mind at ease.

The very next to last number on her recently called list was Matt's. She had a few friends, but she never gave her cell phone number out to anyone unless they factored heavily in her life. Matt had called her two months ago to give her clues as to what Paul wanted for his birthday. And that was the only time he had ever called her.

The phone rang three times before a sleepy voice came on the line with a perfunctory, "Hello?" Matt then launched into a coughing fit, which culminated in a heavy moan.

"Oh, dear! You're not sick too, are you?"

"Linda? Oh my God! Linda!" Matt sounded like a man who had been trekking across the desert and had just been confronted with a priest bearing water.

"Matt. I'm sorry to call so early . . . wait . . . it's three hours later there. What are you still doing in bed?"

"It was a late night last night." He sneezed, coughed twice. His voice had that deep husky sort of tone that one might get from a night of debauchery.

"Listen, I called because I haven't heard from Paul. I've called him and mailed him. But I don't get any answer." There was a prolonged silence while Linda tried to get a grip on her rampant emotions. "I'm scared."

"Linda, listen . . ." He broke off, trying to find a good clear voice to tell her what he needed her to know. "Paul has a few problems just now. And I don't mean that like in the bullshit way a guy has of breaking up with a girl. He has real problems. He's in trouble."

"Trouble? Paul?" She shivered and choked. "What sort of trouble, Matt?"

Matt sighed and lit a cigarette. "Paul would kill me if he knew I was telling you this. Some cops came to see me last night. They said that they found our car at a SuperMart somewhere in CrapSplat Kansas. There was a dead guy in the back seat and the car was covered in blood. They don't know whose blood. Anyway, Paul was nowhere to be found and they're looking for him all over the place." He listened as Linda fell apart and decided not to tell her that the body had been partially eaten.

Linda wailed and screamed, her tears washing over her face, soaking the sheets that she had clutched around herself. Cold didn't just seep into her, it slammed into her, nearly making her pass out. "How . . .?"

"Listen, we don't know what happened. But we know Paul. And Paul is no killer. So, we have to assume that somebody attacked Paul . . ." and he heard her tumble into insanity again. He waited for the return trip. "Somebody probably attacked him and whoever that dead guy was. And Paul probably ran off. We don't know. We just don't know."

"Matt, what if . . .?" She couldn't say the rest. As long as those words went unspoken, everything would be all right.

"Like I said, we have no idea what happened. But Paul's like a brother to me and whatever happened, I'm going to be his friend. I'm going to hope for the best. And I'm damn sure not going to believe that he's dead until they show me a corpse."

And Linda collapsed once more in a fit of tears, beating the bed, tearing at the covers until she thought they would rip apart like her mind had done. When at last she had recovered enough to speak, she sniffed loudly every few words. "You're right, of course. Paul would never do anything to hurt anyone. He must have escaped. Someone attacked him and that dead guy, and Paul managed to escape. And as soon as he can get himself sorted out, he'll call one of us. Let me know right away if you hear from him, okay? And I'll do the same."

"Of course. You know I'll call you right away." He swallowed hard and tried to think of something reassuring to say to her. "Hey, this will all get fixed, ya know? But listen, the cops are probably going to pay you a visit, too. Paul was on his way to your place when this happened. If there's any way in hell he can pull it off, he's going to make it there, too. So, watch your back and keep an eye out for Paul."

"Yea, Matt. You too. And thank you."

"For what?"

"For being such a good friend to Paul. And for being honest with me. I appreciate that."

"No problem, Linda. Later."

She clicked off the phone and only then did she realize that her tears had all dried. That one fact made her throw herself to the bed and start crying all over again.

Milligan was just hanging up the phone when Starnes came in. He clutched in his hands a small stack of papers and sported a smile.

"Hey, Milligan, we got the lab reports back from that car they found in Kansas." He tossed the stack of faxes on Milligan's desk and dropped into a chair.

Milligan picked up the papers, frowning as he scanned them. "So, the blood all belongs to our vic and the fingerprints in the blood match our missing car-owner."

"Yep. What do you suppose happened to the guy? Do you think he killed his pal there? Or was there a third guy and this dude just managed to get away from him?"

Milligan rocked slowly in his chair and thought for a moment. "Well, by all accounts, this Paul Tremblay was a pretty rock-solid guy. Had a steady job with the city, never late, never missed a day. He pays his bills on time, never had any trouble with the law. Hell, he's never even had a speeding ticket."

"So, what do you think happened, then?"

"Well, the way I see it, Paul Tremblay was on his way to Cali to see his girlfriend. And he stopped at this SuperMart to get some coffee or something and that's when the killer shows up. Now, I'm not sure whether the killer put the dead guy in the car or whether he killed him in there, but it looks to me like the guy was slaughtered right there in the back seat. Or . . ."

"Yea? Or what?"

"Or, the dead guy tried to jack Paul's car and Paul killed him by accident. But that doesn't explain why part of the body was eaten. Paul Tremblay's no flesh-eater, that's for sure."

"Then who?"

The cell phone on Milligan's desk rang then, and he reached for it, checked the number but didn't answer. "I dunno. And we won't have any answers until we talk to Paul Tremblay. God knows where he is now. Maybe the killer dragged him off and he's either dead now or . . . worse."

"I wonder who the corpse is." Starnes chewed absently at his nails, a habit he had fought against since he was a child.

"Not sure. The boys in Kansas had to send the body to Topeka to be properly autopsied. We'll have to wait to get the results. And in the meantime, we need to talk to this Linda. She's all over Paul's cell phone and according to his best buddy—who may or may not be the most stoned person I've ever met—Paul intended to marry the girl. If anybody knows where Paul is, it's her."

CHAPTER NINE

Paul peeked out the crack of the door once more. The sun had fully set and darkness had gobbled up most of the town around him. Most, because there was a huge arc-sodium lamp that lit up a basketball court across the street and down two blocks. Save for that one patch of near-daylight, the town was obliterated.

He shuffled back to the kitchen then, intent on grabbing the rat from under the pot and gaining some strength and mental agility to boot. His pockets were filled with useful things: sticky notes, a pen, a pocket knife, the flashlight. As much as he hated to admit it, he was a fully-prepared car thief.

The rat was still bouncing around beneath the pot, trying to find some chink in its armor and make an escape. Paul knew that the thing would bolt the minute he lifted the pot, so he simply slid the pot to the edge until there was enough of a gap for the rat to drop into his waiting hand.

He stuck the poor thing's head into his mouth and bit down hard. For a dead guy, he had some seriously good teeth. The rat was devoured in a matter of two minutes, and Paul was cleaning his hands on a filthy rag that he supposed used to be a dish towel.

He had no idea how far he had to walk, but as he stepped outside, he felt strong and capable. Thoughts flew through his mind then, as he figured out how to accomplish his goal.

Even at nine, there was hardly anyone around to see him. The steady thump of the basketball down the street had silenced some fifteen minutes ago and so Paul was all alone with the tiny dark town. He assumed that he should walk west, the same direction he had been headed before he'd stopped at the SuperMart. He had never been any good at directions. If his car hadn't had a GPS, he'd never have gotten anywhere.

He mourned the loss of the car; felt bad for the sacrifice that Matt had unknowingly made. In a long list of regrets and debts, Matt was at the top.

Paul put one foot in front of the other and plodded along.

He had been walking for over an hour, watching as the buildings thinned out, as the traffic slowed to a trickle and then disappeared altogether. Now, subdivisions sprawled out before him, little dots of light marking each house, each family, each happy life. Paul wondered if he would ever have a happy, safe life again. And he walked.

An hour later found him in the farmland of his dreams. These were small farms, no sprawling corporate entities yet. Privately owned farms meant privately owned equipment. Surely he would find a battered but usable truck somewhere in this agricultural wonderland. His head had become fuzzy again and his legs seemed heavier than when he had started out. His rat was wearing off, he guessed.

The air out there smelled different. It was cleaner and fresher, though there was a back-scent of manure and pesticides. Paul didn't breathe anymore. But through some cruel twist of fate, he could still sense smells. His body had become some sort of bio-mechanical robot, thinking and moving under its own power, but weakened and hard to manipulate.

He heard a sound then, and he stopped in his tracks. All the human residents might have been asleep, but there were still a few pigs on the prowl. At once, Paul's stomach lurched and knotted. The rat he had eaten two hours ago didn't seem to have stuck around long. He wondered, then, what happened to the rat that he had put inside his rotting body. He didn't seem to have any form of digestive system. Had it just dissolved somehow? Would its bones stay in there or be passed out of his body in some manner? These thoughts disturbed him and he grimaced, clutched at his stomach.

The pigs snorted and rooted. They made stamping sounds in the mud. Paul followed the sound until he found them, happy in their little pen at the very farthest side of the property. The farmhouse was some two hundred yards away. Paul squatted behind a copse of trees and watched the pigs, wondering. He remembered seeing one of those CSI type shows once where they used pigs to demonstrate and test different chemicals and weapons. They said that the pig and its flesh were most like that of a human.

If nothing else, the pig must surely give him more bang for his buck than a stupid rat. Since the tragedy that had befallen him, he had put together something of a hypothesis. Human meat repaired his body quicker, helped it stay healed longer. The fresher the meat, the longer it lasted. It was like doing drugs, he mused. The better the dope, the better the high. He eyed the pigs, conjuring images of the greased pig races from the county fairs. He also remembered that pigs were vicious and could kill a man. He would have to be careful.

As quietly as he could, he crept to the edge of the pen and climbed onto the top railing of the enclosure. There were about a dozen pigs in the pen that night, two of them quite small. He doubted that he could take on a full-grown pig on his best day—and this sure wasn't his best day. So, he selected the smallest of all the pigs, and he waited.

It didn't take long before the rutting, mud-covered little pig worked its way around to where Paul sat. As it came directly in line with him, he leaped, landing on the pig and scaring it into a squealing fit. It tried to pry itself loose from his grasp, dug in its cloven feet, and tried to squirm away. The pig was much stronger than Paul had anticipated, and a lot more slippery. Twice, he nearly lost his grip on it, the bottom half of his body sliding into the mud and his feet scrambling for purchase.

But then he dug his teeth into the soft, meaty flesh right behind the pig's ear. Blood spurted—much more than he had counted on—and a piece of flesh tore away from the pig. He swallowed it without chewing, panicking briefly as the hunk of meat lodged in his throat. Several gulping swallows later, it went down.

Another bite and another. It seemed like such a waste to kill a pig and only eat a few bites. And when he could eat no more, Paul pulled out the pocket knife and began to cut long strips of flesh from it. These he stuffed into his pockets, having no other way to carry them. All the other pigs had run off to the corner farthest from Paul and were eying him with something akin to a homicidal glare. Paul climbed out of the pen, wiped the knife on his pants, and put it away.

There was a large barn some fifty feet from the pig pen, and a smaller one just behind that. Paul made his way through the darkness, keeping to the edge of the trees so he could make a fast escape if he needed to. When he reached the smaller of the two barns, he found it unlocked and so he was able to slip inside unseen.

Just as he had hoped, there were two trucks inside that barn. The first was large and new-looking. The second was a good deal older and war-weary. It appeared to be from the early 80s and was pocked with rust and dents. Paul chose that one, since its owner would be less likely to report it stolen. At least, he wouldn't rush to report it stolen. Paul checked the door, found it unlocked, and climbed inside.

It didn't take him five minutes to strip the wires and connect them. These older vehicles didn't have security features the way the newer ones did. The engine choked to life and the gauges all came on. Paul smiled and went to open the barn door so he could drive through.

"Milligan here," the detective sighed into the phone.

"This is Davis, over in Lebanon, Kansas. Listen, we got that autopsy back."

Milligan sat up straighter in his chair and smiled. "Give it to me straight, pal. Don't hold back."

"Well, the vic is one Dana Manning. He's from Chicago originally, but he's been drifting in years past. As far back as age eleven, the kid has been in trouble with the law. He did a stint in the Illinois prison system for armed robbery, then slipped into carjacking. He's got a rap sheet as long as my arm. According to the coroner, the guy was killed when somebody ripped out his carotid artery . . . with their teeth. Apparently, this kid Tremblay has perfect teeth because he's never been to the dentist. So, we don't know if he's the eater or not."

"I'm guessing not. It's just doesn't fit. By all accounts, this guy is squeaky clean."

"I agree. The fingerprints we got off the car match this Manning guy and Tremblay. There are a couple from the other owner, Matt Cassidy."

"Cassidy's alibis all check out. There's no way he was in Kansas when the murder was committed. Besides, he's too stupid to pull it all off."

Davis laughed, perhaps a bit too long. "What about that phone I sent you? You come up with any other prospects who might tell us where our boy, Paul, is?"

"Just one. Apparently, he has a girlfriend on the west coast. Probably one of those online romances, you know. I wouldn't make too much of it. Still, his emails and text messages say that he's heading her way. Somebody needs to talk to her and find out what she knows."

"If old Paul does show up, it's going to be at her house. Yeah." Davis was quiet for a moment, then he chuckled. "Well, I guess I'm going to Californ-eye-ay."

"Want some company?" Milligan was smiling. He licked his lips.

"Well, I don't mind telling you, I'm in over my head with this one. Bring the phone with you and we'll go see what we can see."

"Yes."

Milligan hung up the phone and then started doing the paperwork and making his travel arrangements. His best friend and old Army buddy, Clint, lived in Los Feliz. With a little luck, they could wrap the case and still have enough time before his flight out that he could spend a little quality (bar) time with old Clint.

It occurred to Paul as he drove along in the battered truck that if things had turned out just a little differently for him, he might have made a great criminal. He had stopped at a rest stop some fifty miles ago and exchanged license plates with another truck, whose owner had gone into the rest room. There was no way to disguise himself, but he could trick the cops into ignoring the truck. To that end, he also removed all the logos from the body of the truck, exchanging the front and back one with the truck he had taken the plates from. The Chevy C-10 was now a Ford, for all intents and purposes. Paul smiled, pleased with his cleverness.

The tank had been nearly full when he'd stolen it, but that old truck ate up gas at a frightening rate. Four hours later, Paul was pulling into a small independent gas station. It had automated pumps and so he wouldn't have to go inside, something he considered to be a plus. He gassed the truck and was nearly done filling the tank when another car pulled in on the other side of the pumps. A single man stepped out of it, his face haggard from a night of driving and his head completely bald. The car he drove was a nice new Camry, and he didn't lock it when he went inside.

"In for a penny, in for a pound," Paul sighed.

He put the nozzle back on the pump and opened the truck's door. Then he simply leaned over, grabbed the GPS off the dashboard of the Camry, and drove away. The truck blasted a few clouds of gray smoke as he went, but it accelerated nicely and was around the corner before the guy came out of the station.

Paul drove as far as the next rest stop, and then he drove two miles farther. There was a dirt road which wound its way back into the woods for some distance and Paul turned left onto it. He backed the truck up into a stand of small trees and cut the engine. He didn't want anybody to see the truck sitting by the side of the road but he had work to do.

The pig that Paul had eaten had filled him nicely and—even five hours later—was still keeping him vital. Meanwhile, the rest of the pig meat he had stolen was going stale on the seat next to him. Even that wouldn't last him forever. So, Paul began to make notes. On one sticky note, he wrote,

GOING TO LINDA'S IN LA. On another, he wrote, *YOU ARE WANTED FOR MURDER.* Still another read, *AVOID THE COPS.* And so it went. Every single thing that was important for him to remember was written on a sticky note and pasted on the dashboard of the car. He included instructions on the hot wiring, phone numbers, addresses, and the whereabouts of the ring he had bought for Linda.

When he was sure that absolutely everything of importance was posted somewhere on the truck, he drove back onto the main highway and kicked the truck up to seventy. It shuddered but complied. Kansas was behind him.

The plane touched down in LAX at ten. By eleven, Milligan was zooming along the freeway, his rented car trapped in the fast-flowing sea of traffic. The GPS would guide him to the police department, where Davis had told him to go. Davis had beaten him there by several hours and the plan was that they—together with the LA detective in charge—would go to Linda's house to interview her. Milligan was already growing weary of the traffic and smog by the time he pulled into the parking lot of the LA precinct. He didn't understand how his buddy, Clint, could stand living here.

"I'm supposed to meet Detective Davis and a Detective Lopez here," Milligan told the desk officer. "We're working a case together."

"I'll take you to Lopez," the sergeant said with a sigh.

"Thanks," Milligan grumbled as he followed the man into the precinct offices.

Lopez was a middle-aged, hard-nosed detective of Mexican descent. He had come up through the ranks from the streets, where most of his friends had turned out to be either gang-bangers, or dead. He had soft brown eyes and an easy smile. Life was good for him. Better than he had hoped it could be.

He stood quickly when Milligan came through the door, that easy smile leading, a handshake following. "This is one hell of an interesting case you've got here, Milligan. I don't mind telling you, I had to fight three other detectives to get it."

Davis laughed then. It was disingenuous and shrill. "I fought NOT to get it. Sadly, I'm the only horse in a one-horse town."

Lopez and Milligan exchanged amused glances, and Milligan took a seat next to Davis. "So, I guess the big guy here has filled you in?" The big guy reference came from the fact that Davis was as wide as he was tall. He had floppy jowls that shook when he spoke and hands whose fingers could only barely separate due to the fat on them. That, coupled with his farm boy attitude, might have led most people to think he was slow. Nothing could be farther from the truth.

"Yea, I get the gist. Dead guy in the back seat, half eaten. Owner and driver missing, his fingerprints all over the door. Sounds to me, though, like this Manning guy needed killing. Not exactly a model citizen, was he?" Lopez was gathering things as he spoke: cell phone, keys, walkie, his cuffs.

"Still, we need to know what happened." Davis frowned. "We've never had a murder in my town before."

Lopez slid the small stack of pictures across his desk and spun them to face Davis and Milligan. "You still haven't, Davis. From the condition of the body, the body temp when you found him, the lividity . . . I'd say that guy had been dead for at least 30 hours before he hit your little town. He may have been killed in that car, but he wasn't killed in your town."

"Lopez is right," Milligan agreed with a nod. "It's possible that the car was jacked, Manning killed, and then the whole crime scene was driven to the SuperMart."

"Well, let's go talk to this Linda. Maybe she knows something that will help us find Paul Tremblay." Lopez gave his keys a shake. "Anybody mind if I drive?"

The meat beside Paul had begun to smell. If he had had any choice in the matter, he would have tossed it out the window. But he still needed it. On those rare occasions when he actually had to go inside and pay for gas, he needed a bite of that meat to look normal. And he was saving the very last big chunk of it for when he reached Linda. The note on the rear view mirror said so.

Another note warned him to keep away from the cops, but he couldn't remember why until he saw the note telling him that he was wanted for murder. MURDER! The word was deep and ominous and it scared him. In all his life, he had never thought of killing anyone; had never hated anyone enough to even wish they were dead. And yet, the note said that he had killed someone.

Paul's skin had broken out in a rash of those pustules. They were black and oozing and they smelled. He avoided looking in the mirror because his own face frightened him. That's why he was saving the last piece of meat for Linda. He wanted to look normal just long enough that he could explain to her what had happened and how much he loved her. Then, he would just slip away and die, letting Linda have a nice, normal life with someone else. He loved her enough to do that much for her.

He remembered their second date. She had barely agreed to go out with him in the first place and he hadn't blown it on the first date. So, he had wanted the second date to be special. Beyond special. He wanted it to be the most romantic, amazing, epic date of all time.

The senior dorm building was five stories tall and its roof looked out on the entire campus, plus half of the surrounding city. Paul had spent two days in between work and classes, hauling things up onto that roof. By the time he was finished, he had set up the perfect restaurant vignette with a table, two chairs, some potted trees and plants. He strung Christmas lights everywhere, brought up a stereo, even went so far as to get one of those fire pits and some fire wood. He put a loveseat in front of the fireplace. If Linda wasn't in love with him at the end of that date, it wouldn't be for lack of trying.

So it was that on a clear night with a star-speckled sky, Paul brought Linda to the top of their world. He was wearing a tux at the time, she a powder blue chiffon dress that looked like it had been stolen from the fifties. She was gorgeous. The look on her face when she saw the set-up was incredible. And she'd grabbed Paul around the neck, kissed him hard, and hugged him until he couldn't breathe.

"You did all of this?" she asked softly. "For me?"

He nodded dumbly and smiled. "And to keep that look on your face, I'd do it every night for the rest of my life."

Tears had gathered in her eyes and she had kissed him again. From that moment on, she was in love with him. The moment she took her first bite of his cooking, she was his, lock, stock, and barrel. No other man stood or would ever stand a chance with her. She was Paul's Linda.

Paul almost ran off the road thinking of that night. The sobs shook him hard and though his heart no longer beat, it broke. She had taken him back up to that roof three weeks later and they had made love on a Flokati rug with the fireplace burning brightly next to them. They had rolled themselves into a Flokati burrito and slept there, in each other's arms.

He almost couldn't go on. It occurred to him that Linda should remember the good Paul, the handsome Paul, the romantic Paul. Not the decaying corpse of Paul that he had become. Perhaps this whole thing had been a mistake. Perhaps he should just go curl up somewhere and wait to return to the earth.

Still, she had to know. She couldn't spend the rest of her life searching for him . . . for what they had been together. He reached out and turned on the radio, hoping for some happy music to cheer himself up by. He searched the channels, found a lot of religious stations, one oldies station, and a top-20. He kept the dial there.

The miles were rolling by slowly . . . too slowly. When Paul looked down at the speedometer, it said 35. He was doing thirty-five in a seventy zone. Grumbling, he pushed down on the accelerator and felt something in his ankle give. He hoped that something wouldn't prevent him from walking when it came time to get out of the truck.

He was close now . . . so close that he could almost feel Linda.

CHAPTER TEN

The three detectives stood outside of Linda's apartment, Huey, Dewey and Louis with gold shields. It was Lopez's jurisdiction, so he took the lead, wrapping lightly on the door and then stepping back in line with his fellows. The door creaked open and an eye appeared, blinked, dulled.

"Linda Gilchrist?"

"Yes?"

"I'm Detective Lopez of the LAPD. This is Detective Davis of the Lebanon, Kansas police department, and Detective Milligan of the NYPD. We'd like to have a word with you, if we could."

Suspicion eclipsed the normally soft lines of her face. It hardened and her jaw set. It was obvious that she had been crying. "Is this about Paul?" Her voice cracked, choked.

"Yes, ma'am, I'm afraid it is. Could we come in?"

She pushed the door further shut, then took off the chain and flung the door wide open. "Of course, sir. Please come in."

The apartment inside was something out of a time-warp. It had been decorated in the sixties which, Lopez figured, was the last time they had renovated the building. There was orange shag on the floors in the living room, orange and aqua linoleum in the entry and the kitchen. The walls wore flocked and Mylar paper; the curtains were mostly beads.

Linda noticed their expressions and she smiled. "I rented the place furnished. It's all I can afford until I get tenure."

They nodded in unison and followed her slowly to the sofa. It was upholstered in crushed velvet and it dragged at their pants as they sat down.

"How long have you known Paul Tremblay?" Lopez asked, taking lead.

"Oh, I've known him ever since college. That's when we started dating and fell in love. We lived together for a while in New York. And he's going to join me out here as soon as his job for the city is done. Was. Was going to join me." She looked like she might cry then and all three men shifted uncomfortably on the sofa.

"So, it's safe to say that you know him better than anyone?" Milligan played with the crease on his trousers. The heavy velvet upholstery was making him sweat.

"Yes, I think so. Paul and I are very close. We talk a couple of times a day on the phone . . . or we did until . . . you know."

"Ma'am, when was the last time you heard from Paul?" Milligan felt sorry for her, he really did. But he needed answers.

"Well, let's see . . . it was three days ago. We didn't really talk, because he was sick and had laryngitis. So we texted. And he emailed me to let me know what was going on."

The three detectives exchanged glances, then Lopez took a chance. "Would it be possible for us to read that email? Would that be okay with you?"

She nodded but didn't move to stand. For a moment, she looked as though she might collapse, but then she suddenly shot up off the sofa and walked to the foyer table. When she came back, she was holding the cell phone out to him. "This is the email he sent me. You can actually look at anything on the phone you want to. I don't have any secrets."

Lopez took the phone and the three of them scrunched together to read the email. When they were done, Lopez passed the phone back to her with a thin smile. "Do you have any idea at all what happened to him at work? He talks about it changing him forever."

"No, I haven't a clue. I'm so stunned by this whole thing. See, I thought he was at home and sick and then he tells me that he was really driving out here the whole time. I spoke to his roommate, Matt, and Matt said he couldn't tell me everything that was going on. He just told me that Paul's car had been found in Kansas with a body in it and it was . . ." She fought back a rising gorge, her eyes closing with the effort and her face paling. "Is this true?"

"I'm afraid so, Ma'am. I wish I could tell you more than that, but I can't." Lopez gave her his most sympathetic look. Truth be told, he wanted to give her a hug. She looked like she needed one very badly.

"I understand. But I have to tell you, Paul Tremblay is the kindest, most gentle, caring man I've ever met. And that's not just blind love talking. It's a fact. Ask anybody."

"Yes, ma'am." Milligan let her run with it. She needed to get it off her chest and he meant to let her.

"He would never kill anybody. Never. No way. He can't even eat a lobster or a crab because he says it makes him feel uncomfortable the way they stare at him."

"We're not sure what happened, ma'am," Lopez continued gently. "There's still a good chance that Paul is alive and well. But we need to find him so we can know what happened. He's coming to see you and if he makes it, that's our best chance to talk to him. So, if he calls, emails, shows up here . . . you give me a call." He handed her his card with a smile.

"Oh, don't worry. I will." She tucked the card inside her cell phone case. "One other thing. I get the feeling that Matt is keeping something from me. He was with Paul every single day on the job. If something happened to Paul at work, Matt knows about it. But he won't tell me."

"I understand and we'll be talking to Matt again. Whatever we find out, we'll share with you if you'll agree to do the same."

"Absolutely."

"All right, then. Thank you for your help, Miss Gilchrist. And if you think of anything or if Paul shows up here, you can reach me on my cell phone. The number's on the card." Lopez offered his hand and a smile.

She showed them to the door and the three men tipped their imaginary hats to her as they left, walking down the sidewalk slowly and leaning in to talk.

"You're just going to trust her to call us if he shows up?" Milligan snorted.

"Not a chance," Lopez laughed. "I'm going to put a man on her right away."

For some reason he couldn't begin to explain, Paul had become obsessed with whistling. It had started when he tried to remember the song that had been playing the night that he had taken Linda to Tavern on the Green for her birthday. He had saved up for a whole month for that dinner because she had told him the story of when her grandmother had taken her there when she was little. She had made over the food, the atmosphere, the service, and of course her grandmother's stories. So Paul had gotten the reservations for her birthday, reserved the perfect table. And in the middle of the meal, a violinist had strolled up to them and started playing.

Linda had said the song was the most beautiful song she'd ever heard and now Paul couldn't remember how it went. It was the theme from *Love*

Story he knew, but the tune eluded him. He had begun trying to whistle it, found that he couldn't whistle a lick, and had spent the last hour and a half trying.

The speedometer had dropped again; this time to forty. He pushed down, carefully, and made the truck speed up. He didn't want to attract attention by driving thirty miles an hour under the speed limit.

Three more sticky notes had appeared on the dashboard. One alluded to the birthday-Tavern on the Green-song memory. The other two were in reference to the buttons on the GPS and how they worked. The gas gauge was edging toward "E" again, so he knew he would have to stop for gas.

Paul looked in the mirror and cried out. His lower lip had dropped a good two inches and his right eyelid had begun to droop. There wasn't a square inch on his face that wasn't covered in those hideous pustules, and his hair had begun to fall. That, he had noticed when he ran one hand through his hair and drew it back with a healthy clump of hair—and scalp as well—clutched between the fingers. It had sent him into another sobbing fit.

He studied the exit signs, hoping for a nice, small, automated station he could fill up at. He was so horrible in his countenance now that he couldn't escape notice. The hoodie no longer protected him and he had to wear gloves to hide his green and black hands. There were still two pieces of pig meat rotting beside him on the seat. He thought to take a bite of one of them in order to pass for human at the next gas station.

As it happened, the meat wasn't necessary. When he pulled up to the station, there wasn't a soul in sight. Minimal lights burned, one flickering like a disco ball directly over the truck. Paul slipped out of the truck, his eyes trying to focus, scanning the area for approaching cars. Nothing moved.

He slid his card at the pump and pulled the nozzle from its cradle. He stood stock still and stared then, wondering what the hell he was supposed to do with it next. He blinked and stared and looked over the body of the truck. There was a small opening at the back, just above the fender. That must be it, then. He pulled the little door open and removed the cap. While the tank filled, he went back to the cab and wrote on a sticky note. *PUT THE GAS IN THE LITTLE DOOR OVER THE DRIVER'S SIDE FENDER.* He put it on the dashboard right above the radio.

He had been leaning into the truck, intent on forming the words which would keep his truck going all the way to Linda. When he was done, he stood up straight and turned, spinning right into the face of a very tall man with tattoos on his face. Paul screamed and the man screamed and a gun hit the ground. Scared as he was, Paul couldn't remember what the gun was or what it was supposed to be for. He blinked at the man, who, in the face of stark raving terror, backed away from Paul.

He watched the man go, wondering what the hell was wrong with him, and then stooped to pick up the gun. He turned it over and over in his hand, looking at every part, every detail. Still, it made no sense to him. He tossed it into the truck, letting it land softly on the seat next to the rotting meat. Then he went to remove the nozzle from the truck and replace the gas cap. He knew that by the next time he stopped for gas, he might well require a set of step-by-step instructions for gassing the truck.

He climbed back into the driver's seat then, closing the door after him and gripping the steering wheel. Beyond that, he hadn't any idea in the world what to do. He began reading notes, placed there in the order that he had forgotten each one. *CONNECT THE WIRES TO START THE TRUCK. PULL THE STEERING WHEEL LEVER UNTIL IT SAYS "D". PUSH ON THE RIGHT PEDAL TO GO, LEFT PEDAL TO STOP. FOLLOW THE GPS UNTIL YOU GET TO LA.*

He performed all those tasks in order, wondering why the hell he was driving all the way to LA and where the hell he was now. The signs told him where he was. The rest he was left to wonder about until he could stop and read the rest of the notes.

Lopez eased into his seat, a smile on his face and a cup of coffee in his hand. He pulled himself closer to the desk, realized that his belly kept him from getting as close as he used to, and pushed back. "I've got two of my best guys watching the house. If Paul shows up, we'll nab him the minute he steps out of that truck."

Milligan nodded and Davis started to say something, but then his phone rang. He tilted to one side to grab for the phone, grimacing as he leaned on his left arm. "Davis." He listened for a moment, his face darkening as he did so. There was a pen and a pad within reach and he grabbed it, began scribbling. "Uh-huh. Uh-huh. Got it. Okay. Later."

"Everything okay, Davis?" Milligan asked, his eyebrows raised and his eyes hopeful.

"Cause of death was exsanguination. The bastard bled out when somebody bit a chunk out of his neck. The other damage, to his arm and shoulder, was done after the fact. *Long* after the fact." They exchanged disgusted looks, shaking their heads in sympathy for a man who didn't deserve it. "My guy also says that a truck was stolen last night, long about eleven. It was a brown 1982 Chevy C-10, license number AZP-4130. At that same location, the owner of the truck reports that one of his pigs was attacked, partially eaten, and left for dead. Whoever did it took some of the meat with him."

Milligan grimaced and looked away. "So, our boy not only has a taste for human flesh, but for pigs and rotted flesh as well. You think it was the same guy who killed Manning?"

"So it would seem." Davis sighed. "We don't have a lot of crime in Lebanon. For us, this is practically a spree."

"Then, our guy is driving that truck. Could be Paul Tremblay, could be his killer. Either way, we find that truck and we find some answers." Lopez snatched up the phone receiver and pushed a button. "I'll put an APB out on that truck. In the meantime, Milligan can get one of his boys to go interview Matt again."

Milligan nodded and whipped out his phone. He knew just who to call. If there were answers to be had, Gebhart would get them.

Matt was gulping coffee and stomping his boots onto his feet when he heard the knock at his door. In a good week, he would have maybe one person come to the apartment. This past week had sent a steady flow of people his way and he didn't like it. He would be late leaving for work in another five minutes and he hadn't even had anything to eat. He choked down the last mouthful of coffee and slammed the cup down on the table.

"Coming!" he barked, yanking on his remaining boot as he hopped across the living room. "Coming!" he yelled again when the knocking didn't stop.

"Sergeant Gebhart of the NYPD," the face announced as Matt yanked open the door. The chain hadn't been on it as he had been too stoned last night to check it. "I need to have a word with you."

"No way, man. I'm late for work as it is and my boss will fry me if I'm late again."

"Sounds like that's your problem, not mine." He was a large man with a receding hairline and deep-set eyes. His arms looked like he spent time wrestling bears when he wasn't working. That or he slung a pick axe in his off hours. He took a step toward the door.

Matt threw up his arms and stepped back, letting the door bang against the wall as he yanked it open. "Okay, man, but if I get fired, I'm suing the PD." He shut the door and went to his favorite chair, where he sort of slopped into it, slouching down and stretching out his legs like a petulant child.

Gebhart sat on the sofa and flipped open his notebook. He seemed pleased with himself, as though he had won some great battle or other. "You spoke to Detective Milligan a few days ago, regarding your friend, Paul."

"Yes." Matt was about to say something smart-assed, but it occurred to him that they might have heard from Paul. "Has he turned up? Paul, I mean?"

"No. But Milligan interviewed his girlfriend, Linda Gilchrist, in LA. According to an email that Paul sent her a couple of days ago, something happened on the job the last day Paul was here. We were hoping you'd know what that was."

Matt shifted, licked his lips, tried not to look guilty. He failed miserably. "Dude, whatever happened to Paul, I don't know anything about it."

"Bullshit!" Gebhart stared daggers through him. "The way Linda tells it, you and Paul work as a team. You're always together at work."

"Yea, I guess that's right. But I don't know what happened, man."

"Is that so?"

"Yea, that's so. Look, dude, I gotta get to work." He moved as if to stand up, but Gebhart never so much as twitched.

"I'll talk to your boss. Sit down." Gebhart watched as Matt slid back into the chair, dejected and jumpy. "Now, you and Paul were down in the tubes on his last day here, right?"

"Yea, we were. So?"

"Where?"

"Out in the industrial section. There's that pharmaceutical plant out there, and a couple of other factories." Matt started tapping one crossed foot against the other.

"We know that you called an ambulance that day. And we know that Paul was dead at the site. The EMT says that they took him to the morgue. And then, Paul just disappeared."

Matt felt like he was going to throw up. His face paled and he felt a sudden wave of heat and nausea wash over him. He sat up straighter, drew in a deep breath, and finally looked Gebhart in the eye. "I'm telling the truth when I tell you that I don't know what happened. Honest to God."

"Yea? Well, why don't you tell me what you *do* know and then what you *think* happened?"

Matt hesitated, looked around, trying to figure out just how much trouble he was in. He hadn't done anything to Paul. In fact, Matt hadn't done anything at all, and that might well be the problem. "We were in the tubes, like I said. We were running our tests and doing our measurements and such. We got to the end of that particular pipe and there was this heap of trash and shit between us and the last twenty feet. So Paul climbed the trash with the tape so we could measure."

"Did you lose sight of him while he was on the other side of the trash?"

"Yea. I couldn't see him but I could hear him. He was bitching about some nasty blue goo. When he came back over the trash pile, I could see it on him. We went back to the last junction, climbed up the ladder and got the heck out of there. It was quitting time, ya know?"

"So, Paul was okay then? When you saw him come over the trash?"

"Yea, he was fine. And when we got into the sunlight, you couldn't see that shit at all. We were halfway back to the truck when Paul just doubled over and fell to the ground, flopping around like a big old dead fish or something. I called for the ambulance right away, but when they got there, dude said he was dead. They took him off to the morgue."

"That part we got. So, if he's dead, then how the hell is he driving around in your car and playing with corpses?"

"I don't got any idea about that, man. All I know is that a couple of hours later, Paul comes waltzing in here, alive. He had shit all over his face like zits or something and when he talked, it sounded like when your wood chipper gets jammed up. But he was damn sure alive and he didn't remember anything about what happened down in the tunnel until I told him. That's when he decided to go to LA to see Linda. I tried to stop him, told him to call her or something. But he kept insisting. After that, I don't have any idea in hell what happened with Paul."

Gebhart flipped his notebook shut and stood up. "Okay, Matt. I just need you to do one more thing for me."

Matt frowned, screwed up his face as he stood. He had been waiting for the other shoe to drop. This was it. "What's that, dude?"

"I need you to take me out to that sewer tunnel and show me where you were when it all went south."

"Dude! I already told you, I *gotta* go to work." Matt pleaded with open hands and cocker spaniel eyes.

Gebhart stepped around the coffee table and clapped a hand on Matt's shoulder and squeezed. "I'll fix things with your boss, don't worry. Now, grab a jacket and let's go. I'll drive."

He was out the door then, Matt scurrying to catch up, lock the door, and put on his jacket all at once. Gebhart's car was parked out front and it was a police cruiser. Instantly, Matt could feel the eyes of the neighborhood on him. He wished he had a t-shirt that said MATT DIDN'T DO ANYTHING. Not that it would help.

They drove on for a few minutes in silence, neither looking at the other. "For the record, we don't think you did anything wrong," Gebhart said, breaking the silence. "And we're pretty sure Paul didn't do anything wrong either."

"Well, that's good. 'Cause neither one of us did anything wrong. Paul is my best friend in the world. He's like a brother to me, man. And if anything's happened to him . . . I'll just die." Matt began to cry softly, his shoulders hitching with each sob.

Gebhart wasn't good with that sort of thing. He felt bad for the kid, he really did. But he had a job to do. "So, where is this place, exactly?"

Matt swiped a hand over his face, tried to clear his vision. He sniffed and wiped his nose on his sleeve. "Go four blocks down and turn right. You go over the bridge and then when you pull into the industrial park, take your first left and park out behind the old bottling company."

Gebhart nodded and took his turns. He had a natural aversion to anything that existed underground. Even the subways made him nervous. He supposed it all went back to his beat days, when he used to pick up overtime when he could, sitting the subways. By the end of his second year, he had seen just about everything that the underbelly of life could produce.

"Which way?" Gebhart asked as he slid out of the car.

"Right over here. You have to go down here and then walk the rest of the way. You got a tire iron?"

"In the trunk." Gebhart stepped to the rear of the car and unlocked the trunk. He freed the tire iron and slammed the trunk lid with a sigh. God, how he hated going underground.

"Listen, man, I'm not going down there. You can arrest me or shoot me or whatever you want. But there's no way in hell I'm going down in that tube and I don't think you should either."

Gebhart look at him, assessing Matt's determination, and his fear. He was pale and his body language suggested that he might bolt at any minute. "Relax, kid. I'll go down there. You just have to tell me what I'm looking for."

Matt took the tire iron from Gebhart and lifted the sewer lid up and over. "You can't miss it. Walk about a hundred yards that way," he pointed to his right, toward the water tower. "You can't miss the trash heap."

Gebhart stepped to the opening and lowered himself onto the first ladder rung. "I want you here when I get back, pal. If you're not, I'll find you." He let his eyes say the rest.

"Is there any way I can talk you out of this, dude? Seriously." Matt's eyes were soft and pleading. He seemed genuinely concerned.

"I'll be back up in ten minutes. Then we'll go get a sandwich or something, okay?" Matt nodded but his frown stayed put. "I'm buying."

Gebhart slipped into darkness then, and when his feet touched down, they did so with a splash. Gebhart cursed and shook his feet, trying to get the water off his uniform shoes. He unclipped the flashlight from his belt and switched it on. The trash pile was not nearly as far away as Matt had indicated, so he made haste to it and began to climb to the other side.

He slipped twice and finally crested the heap, which was tall enough to leave a mere three feet between its top and the ceiling of the tunnel. Gebhart regretted those extra cheeseburgers as he slid over the top and made his way back down the other side. He promised he'd work out more, get his wind back and maybe lose a bit of that gut. And then his feet touched the floor of the tunnel and he forgot all about it.

He now understood what Matt was talking about. A few feet away from the base of the trash pile was a large blue puddle and it was glowing like a 60s black light poster. Gebhart watched his step closely, making sure not to get any of that stuff on him. He had a collection bag in his pocket, and he pulled it out, peeled it open. It occurred to him then that he had no gloves and that he would never get the thing to close without getting the stuff all over him.

He searched the trash pile, looking for anything he could use to contain a sample without risking a spill or contamination. There was a pudding container in the pile and he used that to meticulously fill the evidence bag about a quarter of the way. Then, he taped the bag shut and tossed the cup away. He checked himself carefully, making damn sure he hadn't gotten any of that blue crap on him. He had no idea what it was, but he knew it was bad . . . bad enough that just getting it on his skin had killed Paul . . . at least for a while.

When he was back on solid ground again, he heaved a sigh of relief, his eyes adjusting slowly and his face twisted with stress. Matt was there, pacing back and forth and his face drooped with relief when he saw Gebhart.

"You okay, man? You didn't get any of that stuff on you, did ya?" He reached over and grabbed the sewer cover with the tire iron, dragging it into place.

"I'm fine. Really. I got a sample, but I managed not to get any of it on me. What the hell is it anyway?"

"You're asking me? Do I look like a chemist?" Matt laughed then. It was a thin, nervous sound and it made him sound slightly insane.

"Let's drop this by the lab and go get some lunch."

"You're sure you're okay?" Matt looked him up and down, frowning, his brow deeply etched.

"I told you. I'm fine. C'mon." He clapped Matt on the back and made for the car, the bag held lightly between thumb and index finger. He opened the trunk and put the bag into a container, labeled the container with a marker, and slammed the trunk lid.

"I'll take you to my brother's place. He runs a little deli on the east side. They make a hell of a pastrami there. You like pastrami?"

"I guess." Matt didn't like much of anything anymore. Not since Paul had gone away. And if Paul didn't come back, he might never like anything ever again.

CHAPTER ELEVEN

Paul could see Las Vegas burning brightly from twenty miles away. It was like someone had opened up the darkness and let the sun shine on that town alone. He still had plenty of gas to make it to the other side, so he could stop in some out-of-the-way desert gas station instead of a big city mart. His face had seemingly begun to melt and, against his better judgment, he had taken two bites of his remaining piece of pig meat. He thanked his lucky stars that he couldn't seem to taste anything because the stuff had gone green and there was the furry beginning of mold on its surface. But the hunger had hit him so fast, gnawing at his insides and making his head—not just his ears, but his entire head—ring. Aside from that, he was afraid that if he waited too long, his decaying body might be too far gone to repair with any amount of meat.

Now, he had a scant half piece of pig flesh remaining. Would it be enough to restore him to normal Paul status, he wondered? Or was he going to need to get some more somehow? He really didn't want to go through another pig slaughter. That aside, there didn't seem to be a lot of farmland in the Vegas area. And Southern California, he knew, was devoted to oranges, tomatoes and the like. Paul sighed and pressed on.

More than anything, he wanted to avoid crowded places, cops, and busy streets. His mind wandered a lot, even with the meat in his belly. So, he took Highway 215 around the city, joining back up with Highway 15 on the other side. He had about fifty more miles and then he would need gas again, seventy-five if he stretched it. His plan was to take Highway 15 until it joined up with Highway 40 going west, then slide in to Linda's place. One more fill-up and he should be there.

He had made notes in one of his clear moments, having studied the GPS and written down each road and each turn he needed to make. Three times he had had to stop and look up Linda's address, but he finally got it right. Now, even if he lost the GPS or it stopped working, he would know where to go and how to get there. One of the notes warned that the cops were looking for him, but he doubted that the APB would extend this far west from Kansas. Besides, he hardly looked like himself. It would take quite the detective to recognize him now, with his drooping face and pock-marked skin.

Twenty miles after he left the 215, he spotted a small gas station in the middle of nowhere. The desert was flat and you could see for miles. Buildings were easy to spot if their lights were on, but it was hard to tell exactly how far away that bright spot in the night really was. He veered off onto a side road, which consisted of little more than a dirt path which had been cleared of all its scrub. Paul was sure they had poured some gravel on the makeshift road at some point, but most of it had been ground into the ruts and divots that the rare falling of rain had produced.

He watched the station carefully as he approached, hoping for no signs of life, for automatic pumps, for a blind attendant. The setting sun had turned the desert into a cold, barren place, where the chill seeped all the way into your bones and nestled there, like some sort of a parasite. Paul shuddered and pulled up to the pump. There was a sound like a loud bell as his tires crossed a pressure switch and it made him yell in surprise. His mind shot back to a time, long ago, when he had been a little boy and had ridden with his dad to the filling station to get his bike tires tended to. There had been a hose across each pump lane and when you ran over it, a loud bell rang, alerting the attendant of an incoming customer. There were no more attendants, of course, and thus no more bells.

But things here in the far-away of the desert were different on a lot of levels. The bell had damn sure rung and now a short, grizzled man who looked far older than he must be trotted toward the truck. Paul flipped his hoodie into place and tried to avert his face.

"Evening, mister. What can I do for you today?" Despite the location, the man's accent was deeply southern, approaching a drawl.

Paul coughed and made as if to hold his throat, then he flipped out a sticky note which said: *FILL IT PLEASE.* He waited for what seemed like a thousand years for the man to walk back to the pump, pull out the nozzle, and begin pumping the gas. Paul took every opportunity to cough loudly, to wretch his gut as though he were about to cough up a lung. Not only did it offer a good explanation for him not speaking, but it made the man less inclined to come near.

When the tank was filled, Paul whipped out his credit card and thrust it out the window at the man. He took it and walked slowly away, his face contorted and scratching his head. When the man returned, he handed Paul a clipboard with a carbon copied receipt and a pen. Apparently the digital age had completely passed this guy by. When Paul had signed, they exchanged the clipboard for the credit card, Paul waved, and drove away.

After the distance he had traveled and all he had been through, it was comforting to Paul to know that, in a few short hours, he would be with Linda again. This whole mad adventure would finally be at an end. He could finish his business with her and then turn himself in to the police, tell his story, and hopefully finish up the business of his life, such as it was.

He had never been to Los Angeles, but he had heard stories. Luckily for him, Linda lived in a nice suburban area where the apartments were more like townhouses than skyscrapers. Still, he looked a mess and was a complete disaster in every way. He would need to stop somewhere, eat his remaining chunk of meat, and try to regain some semblance of his humanity. Then he would drive to Linda's apartment where he could . . . where he could . . . He couldn't remember why he had come. He took a second to glance at his notes. There was nothing there covering this particular part of the journey. He knew he had driven out here to see Linda, but he had no earthly idea what he was supposed to do when he did see her. He couldn't speak in any form that she would understand and he didn't have a cell phone to text with, or anything at all with which to communicate with her.

Writing down an explanation would have to be a part of that one last stop. He would pull himself together, clear his mind, and then he would write down everything he wanted to say to Linda. That was the plan, at least.

Linda was on her way back to the sofa, a cup of tea in her hand. She had been reading a stack of papers that her students had turned in and her eyes were sore and red. She stopped briefly in the little alcove halfway between her kitchen and her living room to sip at the tea. So far, she hadn't spilled any of it, which was pretty remarkable for someone as clumsy as she. That's when she saw it. There was a little flash of light through the front window.

There was only one window in the front of her house and it looked out over her quiet little street. Even with the drapes closed, she could see shadows out there and bits of pale light. Linda set the cup down on the end table and went to the window to see what might have caused the flash. There was a dark car parked across the street and directly even with her front door. She couldn't see very well, but there did appear to be two dark forms sitting in the front seat. Cops, she supposed, sent to watch the house in case Paul showed up. They didn't trust her to tell them if he came to her. Neither did she.

She watched for about a minute, through a tiny slit in the drapes. Then she pulled them tightly closed and went back to her tea and papers. Surely, Paul would have gotten there by now if he was coming. She worried that he had been killed by the person who had murdered that other guy. She worried that he had taken off in a panic and was lost somewhere, without his car or his phone. Any number of things could have happened to him and none of them were good. Still, she couldn't help but hope that he wouldn't show up here—that he had gone home.

She turned back to the paper she had last been reading. Some of her students were bright, some not so. This one was brilliant. She smiled as she read it, making notes in the margins and red-penning the few atrocious mistakes. Then she added a complimentary note on the bottom of the last page and tossed it into the pile. She was reaching for the next paper when the phone rang. It scared her so badly that she yelped and jumped.

"Hello?" she said, her voice still ringing with fear.

"Hey, Linda. It's Matt."

"Oh, hi, Matt." At least he didn't sound stoned this time.

"Hey, I was wondering if you'd heard anything from Paul?" He sounded like a child who had become separated from his mother in the mall and was just now approaching the help desk.

"I haven't heard a word, sorry. There are two cops parked outside my door though. I'm not sure whether to hope Paul shows up, or hope that he doesn't."

To Matt, her voice sounded so sad that it made him want to cry. "I know this is all hard for you. It's hard for me too. I just want Paul to be okay, you know? If you hear anything, please let me know? I'm going half-crazy here."

"Matt, can I ask you something?"

There was a long pause, then Matt sighed. "Sure."

"What happened to Paul? He said something bad happened at work. You were with him . . ."

"Linda, look. Paul wouldn't want me to tell you. I mean, it's not my place, you know?" There was another long silence, followed by a heavy sigh. "I guess it doesn't make much difference now."

"It might make a difference to me. I need to understand all this."

"Okay, it's like this. We were down in the tunnels and there was this stuff, this blue, glowing stuff. And Paul got it on him and when we got out of the tube, he doubled over, convulsed, and died. I called the paramedics but he was dead before they got there. They took him to the morgue and told me that they would contact me the next day for arrangements."

"And you didn't think to call me? The man I love died and you didn't even let me know?" She was angry now, the heat of it scorching her face and drawing tears to her eyes.

"There wasn't a lot of time. See, a couple of hours later, Paul came walking in the door. But he looked bad, man. Really bad. Like, he had all these pustules and black marks on his face. And he couldn't talk."

"He said he was sick. He had laryngitis."

"Naw, man. He couldn't talk. All that would come out is this growl and groan and shit. I don't know what happened to him, but he looked like a zombie." Matt broke off, feeling very near tears himself. There wasn't a lot in the world that Matt cared about. Paul was at the top of the list. "I'm sorry about all this. I should have protected him, man. I should have gone in his place."

"There's no way you could have known." She swiped at the tears that trailed down her cheeks. "But I appreciate you being honest with me. And I will call you right away if I hear from him."

"I think it might be a good idea if you had a computer or a pad and pen ready in case he does make it there. Dude can't talk, ya know? He'll need some way of communicating with you."

"I'll set the iPad next to the door. That should do it. You take care of yourself, Matt."

"You too, Linda. Bye."

She clicked off the phone and tossed it onto the sofa cushion. Paul was sick with something and that made her feel a little better about his erratic behavior. It didn't explain away everything, but it explained some. She had no idea what to expect when and if Paul showed up, but there was one thing she knew beyond question: Paul was a good and decent man and she loved him more than life itself. When he showed up—if he showed up—she would do whatever she could to help and protect him.

Milligan sat at Lopez's desk, the cell phone tucked neatly between shoulder and cheek as he jotted down notes in his little ringed pad. Twice, he nodded and dislodged the phone; asked Berghart to repeat what he had just said. In the middle of it all, Lopez walked in with two cups of coffee and Milligan gave up the chair to him.

"Just keep me posted. And call me the second the lab results come in."

Milligan ended the call and laid the phone on the desk, taking a second to jot down a few thoughts on his pad. When he looked up, Lopez was staring at him with a crooked smile on his face.

"What time did you come in?" he asked Milligan.

"Six. I woke up at five and couldn't go back to sleep, so I figured I would come in here and get a head start reviewing those tapes from the security camera." He took the coffee that Lopez offered and blew on it.

"And what did you find?"

"Just as expected. Not a damn thing. Tremblay pulls up in front of the SuperMart, gets out, goes inside. Nobody is with him, nobody goes near the car until the cop walks over to ticket him for parking in front of the dumpster."

"So, that leaves Tremblay driving across Kansas with a dead body in his car." Lopez frowned and shuffled through some papers on his desk.

"Maybe he didn't know the body was back there," Milligan offered feebly.

"Not a chance," Davis said, sliding into the chair next to Milligan. "That thing stunk to high heaven."

Milligan shifted in his seat, turned a few pages in his notebook, smiled. "My guy talked to this Matt character . . . and I do mean character. And then they went together out to the sewer site where the two guys had been working. He managed to get a sample of this blue glop that Matt says his buddy got on him right before he collapsed. He's gonna call me when the lab results are in."

"So," Lopez says, rocking slowly. "These two chuckleheads are out in the sewers doing their thing. And Tremblay steps in this blue glop, as you call it. He gets topside and keels over, the paramedics take him to the morgue. Coupla hours later, he walks right back in the door looking like shit. Then he takes off in their car, headed for LA so he can see his lady. Somewhere along the way, he picks up a dead guy or he kills a guy, and then he eats part of the corpse."

Davis shook his head. "There's no question. The bite marks on the body are a dead-on match for the bite marks on the pig. And we found fingerprints on the barn door handle that match Tremblay's."

"Damn," Lopez sighed. "I was hoping for the girl's sake that this guy was innocent. But apparently, he killed Manning, stuffed him in the back seat, and started snacking on him. Then he killed the pig, ate part of it, stole the farmer's truck . . ."

"And if he sticks to his plan, he should hit LA any time now." Milligan nodded.

"I'm going to let my guys know. They need to be prepared. This guy is some serious kind of crazy and they need to treat him like the homicidal maniac he is." Lopez picked up the phone and began to dial.

Four miles from Linda's apartment there was an abandoned grocery store. It had once been a part of a thriving strip mall, and when it had failed, it had taken the other stores with it. Weeds grew through the pavement now, the streetlights dark and the doors of the place boarded up. You could see the front parking lot from two different streets, so Paul drove around back to the loading docks. He backed the truck up into one of the recessed loading bays and shut off the engine. He had to collect his thoughts and write down what he needed to say to Linda. Then he had to eat his last piece of pig meat and try to restore himself again.

Rounding third, he thought. *Almost home.*

He rummaged around in the glove compartment, found his pen and an old receipt pad. He tore one page from the pad and flipped it over so he could write on the blank side. Then he stared into space. He figured he should start off with the most important thing first, the thing he most wanted her to know.

Linda, I love you.

And then he stared some more. He heard a noise off to his right but it turned out to just be a cat rummaging through a pile of trash in the hopes of finding a meal.

The reason I'm like this is because of that awful stuff I stepped in down in the sewers.

He had never been especially good with words, but they failed him now more than ever. The way he had it figured, in about twelve hours he would be down to, "Og luv u. Og sory."

I died and went to the morgue but then I woke up and I was like this. I couldn't talk and that's why I'm writing everything down.

God, he just wanted her to understand. All he wanted was to be able to die without her hating him for all eternity.

I did kill that guy, yes. But it was an accident. He tried to jack my car.

He tried to think back to the rest area where he had killed that man. Yes, the guy had tried to steal the car. But had it really been an accident? He couldn't remember thinking that he should kill the guy. Then again, he couldn't remember a lot of things now. But he was absolutely sure that the whole incident had been an impulse. Some part of him beyond his control had bitten into the guy's neck before Paul had even had a chance to form a clear thought. It had been as much instinct as a tiger taking down a gazelle.

Please don't hate me. I was so sick and so hungry and I bit into that guy's neck before I knew what i was doing. And that's how I found out that eating his flesh made me normal again. It restored me.

It was the lamest thing he had ever said. No way on earth could he get out of this without Linda hating him and thinking him a monster. No way.

Then I just sort of panicked and didn't know what to do. But I found out that I can eat pig meat and get better, so I guess it's any kind of raw meat.

He stared off into space, unblinking, for about five minutes. His train of thought had derailed and try as he might, he couldn't get it back on track.

I just came here because I want you to know that I love you more than anything in the world. Everything I've done, I did for you.

He wondered briefly if that would endear him to her or make her feel responsible, guilty. His eyes traveled over the notes and he gasped at seeing that one. He shoved one hand into his right pocket and felt around. The ring box was still there.

I bought you a ring months ago and I was going to propose as soon as I moved out here. I want you to have it now. And when you look at it, I want you to remember me, the me that used to be. And I want you to remember that you were the most loved woman in the world. As long as I'm alive, you always will be.

And then it struck him. If he died—not like he'd died before, but if he *really* died—then no one would love Linda.

He started the engine and pulled out of the loading bay slowly, turning on his lights. With new conviction, Paul turned down that one last road that would take him to Linda and which would, he hoped, put an end to his suffering.

CHAPTER TWELVE

Milligan was on his way back from the rest room when his phone rang. He stopped in the middle of the hall, nearly causing two patrol officers to run smack into him. Accepting the call, he mashed the phone to his ear and growled.

"Milligan."

"It's Berghart. I've got the test results back."

Milligan was walking again, trotting along the hall and beginning to pant. "Hang on. Just a second." He reached Lopez's office, where Davis and Lopez were reviewing security tapes, hoping to find the one from the rest stop where Paul had killed Manning. "I'm putting you on speaker phone. I'll never be able to repeat all those big words."

"So, I've got the results from the lab tests on that blue stuff. I'll send them to you in a minute. The gist of it is this: There were a hundred and forty-two separate compounds found in that sample. Everything ranging from petroleum to hallucinogenics to radioactive material. There were also a lot of compounds in there that our lab boys couldn't identify."

"Do they have any idea what that stuff might do to a person?" Milligan asked tentatively.

"Not really. They'd have to test it, I guess."

"So, it's possible that this stuff could be responsible for what happened to our perp?" Lopez added.

"Most definitely. I mean, there's enough crazy-assed stuff in that blue goo to drive a nun insane. If it didn't kill her."

Milligan smiled. "'Crazy-assed stuff.' Is that a technical term?" He chuckled.

"It is now, Milligan. And you can quote me on that."

"Thanks. I owe you a beer when I get back, Berghart."

The email came through then, and Milligan forwarded it to Lopez so he could print it out. "So, Paul Tremblay got into this nuclear waste crap and it turned him into one seriously crazed fruit loop."

"That's about it, I guess." Lopez thought for a moment. "It's entirely possible that he's not dangerous anymore. Or if he is, that it's not his fault. God knows what kind of insane stuff it made him see."

"Still, he's killed one man. Responsible or not, he still has to be treated as a danger." Milligan sighed. He didn't like this, not one bit. "You better make sure your guys protect themselves . . . and Linda Gilchrist."

Lopez nodded. "Due force."

In the wee small hours of the morning, most of LA was still asleep. Sunrise was still a good three hours away and Paul putted along in the truck, keeping just under the speed limit so as not to attract attention. In his right pocket was the ring box and the folded piece of paper on which he had written his message to Linda. In his left pocket was the sample he had taken of the blue goo. He had just swallowed the last mouthful of that vile, festering pig meat and was feeling much better for it.

But as he turned onto Linda's street and looked ahead one block to her apartment, he noticed something that he thought odd. There were two dark cars stopped abreast of one another, four men standing in the middle of the street, talking.

Paul stopped the truck, put it in reverse and backed into the first driveway he saw. He cut the engine and watched. He could see each man holding a paper cup of coffee. Handcuffs dangled from the belt of one man. Cops. There were cops guarding Linda.

Paul started the truck and drove away slowly, so as not to attract attention. He watched his rearview mirror as much as he could, making sure that none of the cops followed. If they were looking for the truck, he was done for. Still, they were looking for a Chevy truck with a certain license number. His truck was now a Ford with a different license number.

Paul turned left and drove two blocks before he pulled over, shaking. He needed to get to Linda before his last meal wore off. The cops were guarding her and he had no way of getting in touch with her. Suddenly, he felt panic rise from deep inside his gut, threatening to make him yack up the last of the meat. He choked it back, began to sob, then forcibly got hold of himself.

He needed a cellphone capable of texting. He knew all too well that if he got a burner phone somewhere, it would take too long to activate. Fingers drumming on the steering wheel, he thought hard about his dilemma.

There was only one answer and he had scant little time to make it happen.

He put the truck in gear and drove off quickly. He had passed a Mega Mart on his way into town. Mega Mart carried iPods capable of texting and they had a coffee shop inside with free Wi-Fi. He could buy the iPod and send a text to Linda, asking her to meet him there. But he had to get in and out of the store before the meat wore off and he started to look like a corpse again.

At that hour, the Mega Mart parking lot was nearly empty. The occasional parent making a diaper run, or flu-patient looking for medication pulled in but that was about it. Paul parked the car at the side of the building, as far away from the lights as he could get. Then he made his way across the wide parking lot and in through the sliding doors.

One leg dragged a bit, his foot suddenly leaden. He supposed it had something to do with the crunch he had heard some time back when he had pushed down on the accelerator. There was nothing he could about it except to compensate with his hip. In this hitching, jerky manner, he made his way back to electronics and, by pointing and nodding, managed to get the clerk to understand what he wanted. She eyed him peculiarly and made a face when he handed her his credit card. But he got away with the whole thing and by the time anyone discovered his face on the security tapes, he would be long gone.

He headed quickly for the front of the store, let the greeter check his receipt, and then plunged out into the cool night air. Where the truck was parked, it would certainly be within range of the Wi-Fi signal. He opened the box, turned on the iPod, and frowned in concentration.

It came fully charged, but the charge wouldn't last forever and the only charger needed to be plugged into the wall. But the thing picked up the Wi-Fi signal like a champ and he began the tedious process of registering it. Of course, he used completely bogus information, but it got the task done and out of his way. Then he had only to input Linda's number. Then he entered the text carefully. It was hard to maneuver his big, floppy fingers over the virtual keyboard, but he made it work.

DON'T TELL THE COPS. THIS IS PAUL. MEET ME IN THE EAST PARKING LOT OF MEGA MART. I'M THERE NOW.

He sat back with a smile and waited for her answer. In his mind, he could see her pulling into the lot, racing across the pavement to him, hugging him. She would forgive him everything once she found out what had happened to him down in that tunnel. She would tell him that she loved him, no matter what, and then she would climb into the truck and embrace him. They would drive off into the sunset together . . .

The sound of brakes squealing in his mind. The ocean was there, where the sun set.

They would drive south, to Mexico, where they would live happily ever after. Yea, that was it.

Bing!

Paul looked down at the iPod. Linda had responded.

BE THERE IN FIFTEEN. I LOVE YOU.

She still loved him. Even after all this, she still loved him. Paul felt like crying again, only this time it was because he was so happy. He shoved his right hand into his pocket, just to check on the ring one more time. The ring and the paper were both still there. Good. In fifteen minutes, he and Linda would finally be together again and they would stay together this time, no matter what.

Except that Linda would never make it there.

Linda grabbed her purse and keys from the foyer table and yanked open the door. The night was cool and she was wearing short sleeves, but she didn't care. She was on her way to see Paul, the man she loved more than anything else in the world. She had never loved anyone else. For her, Paul was IT.

She made it as far as the car before the officer approached her, his face full of good humor. He had apparently just started his shift. The scent of coffee rolled off him like water off a duck.

"Ma'am, might I ask where you're going?" He smiled, just to take the edge off.

"Well, I'm running to the store. I need some . . . um . . . feminine products." She smiled sheepishly, hoping he bought it and would leave her alone.

"I see." He seemed to think this over for a moment. There were only two officers and they were supposed to keep her and her apartment under surveillance. The only way he could do that was if he went with her. "I'll just ride along with you, then."

Stunned, she mulled this over. She could jump in the car and lead the cops on a merry chase, then text Paul and tell him, *The key's under the dead plant. Text me when you get into the apartment.* But they would probably arrest her for obstruction of justice or some silly thing. She wouldn't do well in prison. She looked awful in orange and she didn't want to be anybody's bitch. "Fine," she sighed at last.

She unlocked the car doors and slid inside, wondering what the hell she was going to do. Paul was expecting her and she didn't want him to think she had just bailed on him. As she started the car, she realized the obvious answer. She would have to text him from inside the store and have him meet her during the day, while she was at work and could more easily slip away.

She backed the car out and stopped long enough that the officer could tell his partner where they were going. Then she drove straight to the convenience store on the opposite corner from the Mega Mart.

"I'll just be a minute," she said with a grin. And then she dashed into the store.

She managed to walk all the way around to the back of the store, where the feminine products and medications were. She texted as she went, trying not to let the officer in the car outside see her.

COPS WATCHING. COULDN'T GET AWAY. WILL TEXT YOU DEETS TO MEET ME DURING WORK. LUV U. L

She grabbed a box of tampons and a candy bar as she passed, then hurried to the counter and slid her card in the machine. She was very frustrated and shaken by the whole thing. Being a criminal didn't come naturally to her. Heck, she had never even shoplifted, or eaten grapes from the bag while she was still shopping. She could only imagine how disappointed Paul must be, sitting there in his car, waiting for her. It made her want to cry.

She walked out the door then, the officer still sitting in the car, smiling like a goon. She knew it wasn't his fault. He was just doing his job. But she hated him for it nevertheless.

Paul looked down at his phone one more time, just to make sure he had read the message right. Linda wasn't coming. Cops were watching her. She wasn't coming. Those two thoughts ran through his mind in an endless loop until he thought he would go mad from it. Judging by the blotches on his hands, his meat was wearing off anyway. The best thing to do, he mused, was to go somewhere and wait for Linda to send him another message. Then he could find another meal somewhere and be in fine shape when he met Linda.

To that end, he drove back to the abandoned grocery store and backed the truck into the loading bay, where it couldn't be seen unless you walked right up on it. He would wait there, in the shadow of the broad building, until Linda sent for him. Then he could drive to a place of her choosing and deliver his message of love.

Linda gathered her things for work, tucked the ungraded papers into her laptop case, and drained her coffee mug. She hadn't had more than three hours of sleep that night. She felt like shit and she was sure she looked like it too. There was a meeting at nine with the department heads, one at two with the admissions committee. And at some point, she knew, she had a meeting with one of her students who was having problems with his senior dissertation.

She walked out the door, making sure she had engaged the lock before turning toward the police car. She drew a bead on it, marched straight up to it and leaned on the door. "I'm going to work now. Is one of you going to come with me?"

"No ma'am," answered the driver. "I think you'll be safe on campus. Besides, campus security knows what to look for."

"Okay, then. Have a good day, officer." She smiled her best smile and turned away, walked back to her car.

She backed out of the driveway and drove around the corner, where she eased into a parking space and kept the engine running.

ON MY WAY TO WORK. ALONE. WHERE R U?

She tapped one nail on the phone and waited for a response. One glance in the mirror told her that she hadn't yet been followed. That much was in her favor.

LOADING DOCK OF THE ABANDONED GROCERY STORE ON FIFTH.

She smiled more than she ever thought possible. Aside from the aiding and abetting of a felon, this was damned exciting stuff.

ON MY WAY.

Paul smiled and high-fived the air. He was finally going to see Linda. This awful mess was about to be over. God, how he loved her. And needed her. And . . . well, that part of him didn't work anymore . . .but if it did, he would want her too.

He looked in the mirror, frowned at the blotches and sagging. His hands were a mess and his right leg still didn't work quite right. Like a drug addict, he needed a fix. But where in the hell was he going to find a hunk of meat ready to be eaten in the next five minutes.

A clang echoed across the loading docks as a trash can fell over two bays down. The cat was back and, judging by its desperate searchings, it was starving. Paul eased himself out of the truck cab and left the door open. He needed that cat. There were lots of cats. The world wouldn't miss this one.

"Here, kitty, kitty, kitty," he began, suddenly realizing that the cat heard nothing but a feral growl coming from his throat. He watched as its tail puffed up and it arched its back.

He tried a different tactic then. Having no idea what he smelled like, he at least counted on the leftover scent from the pig meat to guide the cat to him. He stooped down and held out one hand, fingers together as if he were holding food in them. The cat's tail un-puffed and began to sway slowly back and forth as it regarded him. Paul wanted to yell at it, to pounce, but he kept calm and held still.

The cat took one tentative step toward him, making a deep, guttural sound and then stopping. Its whiskers twitched as it sniffed the air and it suddenly walked in a circle. Then it stretched out its neck, taking another step and another. A few more steps and it would be within Paul's easy grasp. He would be merciful. He would kill it quickly.

Then there was the squeak of shocks as a car went over a speed bump, the roar of an engine as it accelerated over it. Paul turned in time to see Linda's car round the corner. The cat screamed and ran off.

"Godammit!" Paul growled.

He flipped the hoodie up over his head and turned his back. The ring and the note were in his pocket and he had to give them to Linda, but he couldn't let her see his face. He heard the car door slam, jumped a little. And then he had to use every ounce of determination he had in order to not turn around when he heard her voice.

"Paul! Oh Paul!" she cried, running toward him. Her arms were open and she was smiling.

He reached out an arm, thrust it out behind him in a STOP motion. She stopped mid-stride and didn't make a sound. Paul thrust the paper out toward her. He gave it a little shake so she would be sure to know that he wanted her to take it.

She walked up to him more slowly then, taking the paper from him with just thumb and forefinger. Her eyes were fixed on the back of his head as he stood there, motionless. And for the first time since all of this had started, Linda felt scared.

She began to read the note and as she read, Paul reached into his pocket and grabbed hold of the ring box. He opened it carefully, then he thrust the ring out behind him.

"Oh, Paul," she gasped, without reading past the first sentence. "I'm so sorry all of this happened to you. Please, won't you turn around?" She looked at the ring then, took the box delicately from his hand. There were some blotches there, black and green spots scattered across his hand like paint splatters. "It's beautiful, Paul. I love it so much. Please, turn around, honey."

He shook his head, refused to budge.

She started to walk around him then, to circle around to look in his face. Paul turned, growled "No," and kept his face from her.

"I love you, Paul, and you have to know that I'll marry you. Of course I'll marry you." There was a lilt in her voice, a girlish joy that made Paul's heart melt and he nearly turned around then.

She tried to dart in front of him but he was too quick. He spun away before she could see his face.

"Paul, honey, I know this all seems so bad. But I love you and I don't care what happens or what you look like, I'll always love you. Please, Paul, turn around. We'll get married right away. I love you, no matter what. And whatever's happened, we can fix it. Together."

It sounded to Paul as though she was going to cry any minute. The pain in her voice broke his heart and he began to turn, slowly, his chin tucked against his chest, his eyes on the ground. He was terrified of how she would react. He didn't want to see the look of horror in her face. But he had to know.

Linda sucked in one last breath of air and held it, watching as Paul turned. She braced herself, gripped the note and the ring so tightly that she feared she would break the ring box. She was afraid to even blink for fear the tears would start flowing.

His face came into full view then and he lifted the hoodie up and away from his face. Linda gasped, clapped one hand over her mouth, and began to shake. It started as a small tremble in her lips, then spread to her head and her hands and finally it took over her entire body. She shook so hard that she dropped the ring and the note.

She took a step back.

And she took another.

Paul watched as, screaming, she turned and fled to her car. He reached out for her, the very worst thing he could have done, and tried to follow her. His dragging leg slowed him down and, in slow motion, she leaped into the car and turned the key.

"Please, Linda! I won't hurt you, I swear. I love you. Come back!"

None of that got through to her, though. In her eyes, a monster was coming for her, reaching out to snag hold of her and growling his hunger. She threw the car into drive and roared past him, taking one last look in the rear view mirror to see Paul standing there, motionless, his head cocked to one side and his arm still outstretched.

And just like that, she was gone.

CHAPTER THIRTEEN

Paul stood there for a very long time, unblinking and numb. Then he walked back to the truck and got in, slamming the door after him. He screamed and raged, pounded his fists on the steering wheel until one of his fingers broke off and fell with a soft thump to the floor. Then he started to sob, great wrenching sobs that shook him through and through.

When he had a chance to calm himself and think things through, he realized that the note and the ring were still outside on the pavement. The wind had caught the note and so it was slowly blowing down the length of the loading docks. He got out right away and began to chase after it, his feet slapping and dragging on the pavement until finally, in desperation, he lunged for it. His fingers managed to slap down on one corner of the paper and he pulled it to him. He collected the ring on the way back to the truck.

What to do now? Linda had been terrified. There was a chance, though, however slim, that she would shake off that initial fear, reconsider, and come back. He sat in the truck for a long time, clinging to that feeble hope. But Linda never came back. She hadn't even read the note and now she would never know how much he loved her.

He would have to try again to see her. He needed to refresh himself, wait until dark, and then go to her apartment. He scrunched down on the seat, trying to stay out of sight in case someone drove around the back of the store. That's when he saw the iPod and remembered that he had it. He snatched it up and turned it on, found Linda's number.

LINDA, I LOVE YOU SO MUCH. I WOULD NEVER EVER HURT YOU. PLEASE, COME BACK AND READ THE NOTE. I'M NOT CONTAGIOUS AND I PROMISE TO STAY BACK FROM YOU. PLEASE.

He waited for what seemed an eternity for her answer. And when it came, he began to weep again.

I CAN'T.

Nothing more. Just "I can't." He stared at it until the words doubled and blurred and finally disappeared into a soft white puddle.

When he had gotten hold of himself and the sobs had faded into light hitches in his gut, he tried to focus on a solution. Linda had to read the note. If she didn't read it, then everything he had gone through was for nothing.

In order for Paul to give her the note, he had to be normal looking. And that meant feeding again. He looked around him, to see if he could spot the cat. The beast had bailed and was nowhere to be found. Paul fixed his eyes on the field, the last place he had seen the cat just as it had disappeared from sight. He kept watching, hoping, praying that the cat would return.

After nearly an hour of sitting as still as a statue, he saw the tall grass beyond the curb move. It rustled a bit and then it began to dance. The cat peeked its head out, its tail dragging low on the ground. It was cautious, ready to turn and run.

Paul let the animal make its way across the parking lot. He waited until it was over by the trash cans where it felt safer and more comfortable. He gave it time to gain courage. Then he slowly opened the truck door and simply slipped down onto the ground. He sat there, cross-legged, not moving, for a good half hour. The cat hid behind the trash cans, looking out every now and again but not making a move. And then, the most miraculous thing happened: The cat simply walked out from behind the cans and straight toward Paul.

Still, he didn't move. He let the cat sniff him, watched as its whiskers twitched and its eyes scoped him out. The tentative cat rubbed its head against his leg, turned, rubbed its way back the other way. If Paul had been of the breathing variety, he would have exhaled just then.

He knew he had one chance and one chance only. If he let the cat slip out of his grasp now, it would never come back to him. He felt kind of bad about the whole thing. The poor creature was hungry and it had trusted him. Despite the stench of decay and the festering sores, the cat had come to be his friend.

Moving faster than he ever thought possible, Paul lashed out with both hands and grabbed hold of the cat. It spit at him and claws lashed out at Paul's hand, but still he held on. It tore great hunks of flesh from his arms and shredded his shirt as he brought the creature to his mouth. He took one giant bite then, directly into the cat's neck where he supposed its artery would be. Blood bathed his hoodie and spattered his face. Mercifully, the cat died instantly.

Paul spat out a hunk of the cat's neck. It was covered in fur and he had almost choked on it, so he spat it away and took a fresh bite from the cat's lean neck. Then, he let it sit limply in his hands for a moment, the blood draining onto the concrete. "I'm sorry," he said in his growly voice, feeling genuine sorrow for having taken the cat's life. But his body felt instantly better. His mind cleared.

He took the cat back to the truck, sitting it on the front seat beside him. He would eat the rest of it right before he went to see Linda tonight, after dark, when things would be easier. He would drive the truck to the block behind Linda's apartment and sneak up to the back door. She couldn't possibly refuse to see him, not when he looked so normal.

He checked himself in the mirror. Skin clear, eyes bright; once he cleaned the blood from his face, he would look like a million bucks. Nothing to do now but wait for dark. Then he would make one last attempt to see Linda.

Linda had been so shocked at Paul's countenance that she had nearly run off the road trying to get away from him. She had made it as far as the Quickie Mart, where she had pulled into the parking lot and put it in PARK. She was crying so hard that she couldn't see the dashboard and her body was trembling.

Paul had looked like a corpse. She thought about that: The way Paul had looked, how he had sounded when she spoke to him on the phone, the blue goo that he had talked about. It wasn't his fault, she knew. He hadn't asked to be like that. Still, he had horrified her with the way he looked. And he had brought her a ring. A ring, of all things!

She wanted to forgive him, to go back and apologize and find some way to help him. She just couldn't stomach it. Not even for Paul. Neither could she turn him in to the cops. She owed him that much.

She wiped her face and cleared her nose, then put the car into reverse. She had meetings at work and then she would buy a bottle of nice, sweet wine and go home. She thought about that term now: home. She had an apartment, a few friends at work, a nice job, everything but Paul. And Paul was not coming back to her, at least not the Paul she had known all these years. There needed to be a new plan for the rest of her life, one that didn't include Paul. The thought of it made her cry again.

She went to the college, walked into her first meeting ten minutes late. The rest of the day, she just phoned it in, getting to her final meeting, managing to hurry it along. Come tomorrow, she might need a mental health day. But for the rest of this day, she managed to hold it together.

It took some thought for her to remember to get the wine on the way home. She grabbed some chocolate as an after-thought, then stuck a pre-fab sandwich into her mix. Now, she figured, she had everything she needed to make it through the night.

The police car was still out front when she got there. She waved to the officers inside and parked her car in the driveway. Even if she couldn't spend the rest of her life with Paul, she wasn't about to give him up to the cops. She got out of the car, grabbing her laptop case and grocery bag from the backseat and locking the car before she went inside. The sun would set in about an hour. She hoped there would be something upbeat and fun to watch on TV. This was not the night to be grading papers.

Linda went inside, pushing the door closed with her butt as she struggled to kick off her shoes. She dropped the laptop off next to the table, and then went to the kitchen to get a bottle opener and a glass. She padded through the house in stockinged feet and collapsed onto the sofa. *Ferris Bueller's Day Off* was on TV. Perfect.

Paul waited until a half hour after the sun had set. He had gotten bored while he sat and did nothing, so he had been picking at the cat meat the whole time. He looked into the mirror and liked what it saw. There was no better time than the present.

He started the truck and put it in gear. Oddly, he hadn't seen another living soul the whole day. Not even the bums came to hang out there, he guessed. Today must be his lucky day.

He turned right and then left and then right again, trying to scope out the backyard and gauge where Linda's apartment was from the back. He knew that it was brick, that it had a tall oak tree on the side. And then there it was. The tree stood a good twenty feet higher than the apartment and its spread offered shade to the side yard of the building adjacent to it. It was a pretty tree, and it seemed to him that it was just standing there, waiting for its tree house to be built. Paul let the car idle.

A cursory glance proved that his method of encroachment would not be as easy as he had thought. There was a fence which separated Linda's apartment from the neighbor's mid-century ranch. It was a six foot fence, made of wood, and it looked fairly new. The fence surrounded Linda's apartment rather than the neighbor's, so he had hopes that there would be no dog standing guard.

He parked the truck and got out, shoving a huge piece of cat meat into his mouth and chewing quickly. He would need all his strength and agility to crest that fence. And he wanted to look his level best when he was face to face with Linda. But as he approached the yard, he realized the error he had made. The wood fence did indeed surround Linda's yard. But there was a chain link fence surrounding the backyard of the neighbor's house.

Inside that yard, watching like a predatory cat in the jungle, was a Rott-weiler. Lying beneath the bushes as he was, even the dog's eyes couldn't be seen. But when he stood up and made a run at the fence—just as Paul had put his hand on the latch—Paul got a clear picture of just how much trouble he was in. The dog stood at least waist-high, his head broad and his chest even broader. And when he leaped, the dog nearly cleared the fence.

Paul took three stumbling steps backward, arms flailing and his mouth hanging slack. The dog strained at his chain link bonds and barked and snarled. Lights came on in the house where he lived and someone opened a door and came out on the back porch. Paul turned to run then, managing to conceal his face before the woman rounded the corner. By the time she arrived at the side yard, the dog now whining and panting, begging for a pat or some food, Paul was back at the truck.

So, no way in hell was Paul going to make it to Linda through the back yard. A full frontal assault was required and he knew no other way to go about it. He walked to the corner, rather than give himself away with the chugging growl of the truck's engine. Then he turned and walked to Linda's street. He was coming at the apartment from the police car's rear, keeping to the natural shadows on the sidewalk and keeping his head down. If he was very lucky, he would get right to her driveway before the cops realized he was there.

He walked briskly, a man with a purpose, a man with a plan. His hands were in his pockets, on the note and the ring box. He had neatly refolded the note and written on the outside a message that he hoped would capture Linda's heart and make her read the letter:

FOR OUR LOVE
READ ME
I BEG YOU!

His plan was to out-distance the cops, make it to the door, and either ring the bell and hope that Linda made it there before the cops, or simply burst inside. Then he would shove that note into Linda's face where she couldn't miss the message outside. Hopefully, that would do the trick.

When he came even with the neighbor's driveway, he heard the dog bark in the distance. No doubt, the cur was still upset by Paul's visit. So was Paul.

The cops notice him as he turned up the driveway. He heard the car door creak a bit as it opened and he hurried his pace. It was no use. The cop was coming toward him now, his face set into a very serious scowl.

"Hey, buddy. Can I talk to you for a second?" The cop waited a beat and when Paul didn't stop, he said, "Hey, pal! Hold it! Stop! Police!"

Now the other car door creaked open. Paul heard footsteps behind him, sensed without looking that the cops were chasing him.

"Stop or I'll shoot!" said the other officer.

Paul was on the front step now and he let his hand flail outward and smack into the doorbell. He turned then and faced the cops. They stopped for a minute, sudden realization stealing their momentum. Their guns came up, both at the same time, aimed directly at Paul. Paul started to raise his hands, the ring in one and the note in the other.

And that's when everything went horribly, terribly wrong.

The sound of the door opening registered briefly in Paul's brain, as did the nearness of the gun-bearing police officers. Then Paul did the worst, most dangerous thing he could have done. Paul Tremblay turned and dove toward the door. His only hope was to stun the police into not shooting him.

Linda had opened the door and she stood there, her mouth forming a tiny "o" as she gawped at the sight of Paul. His sudden leap toward her stunned her as well, though not as much as the cops.

The policemen, who were far too keyed up to think clearly, panicked and opened fire. Paul felt the bullets strike his body and pass through it. He didn't spend any thought on where they went after that. His eyes lifted and he caught the expression on Linda's face just as he fell. His dive had taken him in through the door, but then gravity took hold and dumped him at Linda's feet.

Focused on the task at hand, desperate to complete his mission, he thrust up both hands, the one with the note and the one with the ring. His eyes pleaded. But by the time his brain caught up to his vision, he realized that it was too late. The bullets that had passed through him as though he were made of air had hit Linda in the chest and the abdomen. Her eyes opened wide and her knees buckled. Paul let out a yell as he watched her fall, felt the jarring thud as she hit the tiled floor.

"No!" he yelled in his gruff zombie-man voice, grabbing onto her and shaking her. "No, Linda! No!"

Her head turned and she brought her eyes to bear on him. Blood was leaking from her in four places, covering the tiles and his hands as he clutched at her. He began to sob, his eyes meeting hers, his face a study in misery. "Don't leave me, Linda. Please don't leave me."

And then the most startling, brilliant idea hit him. In his other pocket was the jar full of blue goo. It had killed and then resurrected him. Maybe it would resurrect Linda, too. He reached into his pocket and grabbed the jar, twisting the lid off in one smooth movement. Then, he spread the stuff over her, pouring some in each wound, smearing some on her face, getting it into her mouth. He knew how it would look to the rest of the world, but if it worked, if it saved her, it would all be worth it.

Then Paul took the only out he could. He already had four holes in him. His heart had stopped and he no longer breathed. So, Paul just collapsed on Linda's lifeless body and waited.

EPILOGUE

The two cops would forever talk about that night. They told and retold the story about how they killed the zombie over the next few days, lengthening and embellishing it until there was very little truth to it. The official report that they filed with their superior, however, was far more accurate.

Upon seeing that they had shot not only the zombie boyfriend, but Linda Gilchrist as well, they had run to the doorway to see if they could save the girl. When they arrived, they spotted the man's body, splayed across the girl, both of them dead. There were four holes in the man and four matching holes in the girl. Blood was everywhere.

They found the ring, the note and the jar. In the light of the foyer, the blue goo was invisible, so they had no idea that it was there. But they stuck the other items into the man's pocket and called it in. The two officers were suspended for their grievous mistake, but eventually allowed to return to duty. They spent the rest of their careers as resource officers in the local middle school, breaking up food fights and in general being mocked by snot-nosed punks.

Paul rose first, having lain there for hours, waiting for the attendants to leave. He was far smarter than they would ever have guessed, since he knew damn well that they would think him dead and would send him to the morgue right along with Linda. There were stories circulating and they probably would continue to circulate for decades. But he didn't care.

He turned his head and listened to his neck crackle with the movement. Linda was right there next to him, on the table but not yet autopsied. He stretched then, fighting off an eerie sense of déjà vu. He swung his legs over the edge of the table and he staggered to Linda. Smiling, he stroked back her hair, kissed her gently.

"Wake up, Linda. Come back to me, baby." He waited. He couldn't remember how long it had taken for him to come out of it but he was sure it was longer than a couple of hours.

Her eyelids fluttered then and she peeled them open. The first thing she saw was his face and she nearly screamed with terror. Paul helped her sit up and held her hand while she fought to remember what had happened.

"Where am I?" she asked softly, trying out her new voice and blinking.

"You're in the morgue." He hugged her carefully, and then it hit him. He thrust her out to arm's length, staring at her.

"I understood you. Oh Paul!" She hugged him hard, laughing. "Wait! Why am I in the morgue? What are we doing here?"

Paul looked sad at that, his eyes lowering and his smile fading. "I'm afraid you're dead, honey. Just like me. The cops shot us, remember?"

She screwed up her face in hard thought and nodded slowly. "Did you bite me and make me come back?"

"No! I would never bite you. I just smeared some of that blue goo on you to make you come back. I'm so sorry, Linda. This whole thing is my fault. I should have stayed in New York. It's my fault that you got shot and it's my fault that you're undead."

"Well, it's not like you could ask me what I wanted. I mean, I was . . . dead." She shrugged and slid off the table, testing her new legs and searching the room with her pretty eyes. "So, what do we do now?"

"I suppose we get out of here before they autopsy us. Our clothes should be right under the tables on those little shelves." He looked and, sure enough, there were the bags with their clothes. "Let's get dressed and then we can decide where we're going to go and hang out for the rest of our . . . lives."

She began pulling on her jeans, her little feet popping out the end of the pants legs, toes wiggling. "Do we have to eat human flesh? I don't think I'll like it."

"No, any old flesh will do, as long as it's raw."

"Ew! I hate raw meat. How about sushi? Does that count?"

"I don't think so, but I'm no expert."

She pulled the t-shirt over her head and then slipped into Paul's arms. "Canada or Mexico?" she asked with a grin.

"I think Mexico. It's warmer there."

"But the cold would preserve us," she argued.

"Not really. But before we go anywhere, we need some food." He watched her make a face, pulled open one of the drawers. There was a body inside and Paul smiled. "He's already dead. He won't miss it."

"Won't they freak out when they find us gone?"

"I'm sure they will. You know, it occurs to me that we need a Renfield."

"A what?"

"Dracula had Renfield, a guy who could go out in the daylight and do his bidding, fetch him fresh bodies, and all that. Let's go to New York. We'll pick up Matt and then decide where to go."

"Okay." She smiled at him, trying not to watch as he sliced slabs of meat from the corpse and stuck them in a plastic bag.

When he was done, he closed the drawer and turned back to her. All of a sudden, he snapped his fingers and reached into his pocket. "I almost forgot," he said, sinking down to one knee and holding out the ring to her. "Linda Gilchrist, I love you with all my unbeating heart. Will you marry me and be my wife for as long as we both don't live?"

She clapped her hands together and laughed, taking the ring from him and putting it delicately on her finger. She studied it in the light, watching the sparkle and casting reflections on the wall behind Paul. Then she sank to her knees and took both his hands in hers. "You know I will. I love you, Paul Tremblay."

He smiled at her, his new wife, the love of his life and his partner in the future. She was perfect in every way, not just perfect for him. So, they headed for New York and even after the cops discovered that their bodies were missing, they were hesitant to do anything about it.

AFTERWORD

Paul and Linda grabbed Matt from New York and headed for Mexico, where they would live happily forever after.

Davis, Lopez and Milligan buried the case files in the cold case section. It wouldn't benefit anyone's career to institute a search for two walking dead people. Besides, they were pretty sure they knew what had happened. The pair had been revived and, now that they were together, had no interest in much of anything else. They would be no further danger to the world. Two years later, while vacationing in Mexico, visiting family, Lopez thought he saw Linda at a local cantina. He kept it to himself, and found another place to drink.

About the Author

Patricia Lee Macomber is the former editor-in-chief of *ChiZine*. She has been published in *Cemetery Dance* magazine and such anthologies as *Shadows Over Baker Street*, *Little Red Riding Hood In the Big Bad City*, and *Dark Arts*. Currently, she lives in North Carolina with her husband, David, and their children.

Curious about other Crossroad Press books?
Stop by our site:
http://store.crossroadpress.com
We offer quality writing
in digital, audio, and print formats.

Enter the code FIRSTBOOK
to get 20% off your first order from our store!
Stop by today!

CPSIA information can be obtained at www.ICGtesting.com
Printed in the USA
BVOW040052030613

322155BV00004B/93/P